PARKER CANYON MASSACRE

A SLIM CALHOUN, BULL MORRISON
WESTERN
BOOK 5

JOHNNY GUNN

WOLFPACK
PUBLISHING
— EST 2013 —

Trouble in Pioche
Paperback Edition
Copyright © 2023 Johnny Gunn

Wolfpack Publishing
9850 S. Maryland Parkway, Suite A-5 #323
Las Vegas, Nevada 89183

wolfpackpublishing.com

Paperback ISBN 978-1-63977-708-2
eBook ISBN 978-1-63977-709-9
LCCN 2023940082

PARKER CANYON MASSACRE

CHAPTER 1

Four men dressed in heavy buffalo robes, riding ice caked horses, made their way over Jumbo Grade but could not see Washoe Lake, hundreds of feet below them. Jumbo Grade Road connected Virginia City's mines and mills to Washoe Lake, where timber mills prepared massive amounts of lumber for the mines. Icy winds at near hurricane strength left the ground almost bare but drifts hid deep gulches and ditches full and dangerous. It eliminated any chance of seeing the lake far below. The road from Virginia City to Washoe City was one of the most treacherous in all of the Nevada Territory.

"If that bank down there in Washoe City's warm I ain't robbin' it, I'm settin' up camp there." Jackson Whitmore, a drifter out of West Texas, wanted in more than one territory, shivered and tried to dig deeper into his wool lined point robe. "Them mountains across the valley are the Sierra Nevada. That big one is ten thousand feet high. That's why this wind's so damn cold.

That snow's ten feet deep up on that ridge, I'll sure as hell betcha."

The view would come and go as the wind driven snow allowed and in a straight line was only about ten, maybe fifteen miles distant. Scrub pines and juniper on the Virginia Range, ponderosa pine, sugar pine, and fir in the Sierra. In between, Washoe Lake.

"First he's a crazy gunman, now he's a scienteest," old Crazy Ned Paulson laughed. "I'll tell you what, Whitmore, if they's an iron stove in that bank and it's lit, we'll take turns standing next to it after we kill the banker, grab the money, and make sure there ain't no one alive to tell on us."

Chuckles were mixed with grumbling as the four made their way off what was locally referred to as Sun Mountain. The maps called it Mt. Davidson. Halfway down the mountain's eastern flank was the booming metropolis of Virginia City, home of the fabulous silver strike called the Comstock Lode. These were the building years following the discovery just a few years ago.

The area was part of Utah Territory, but following the immense strike the Mormons didn't want all those non-believers in their territory and didn't object when the district became Nevada Territory.

"I think we can light a fire in that bank if we need to," Sonny Jackson said.

"Why not?" Lefty Lopez joked. "It's a free country, or so I've been told. This ain't no place for a man to have to be, though." He jerked the buffalo robe tighter, snugged up the braided leather belt and tied it tighter. "Why we goin' to Washoe City to rob a bank when there are two banks in Virginia City? And it ain't near this cold in Virginia City."

"Only goin' to say it one more time, boys. I've already said it twice. The bank in Washoe City has county money, lumber mill money, and Comstock mine money. Lots of money. More than the two banks in Virginia City combined. Now, again, I've got this all laid out with Big Maude—we even got us a place to hide out, she said." He stretched some, stood tall in the stirrups, and glared at the men.

"You don't want to ride with me, you should have said so back there." Crazy Ned Paulson let his hand brush aside the heavy buffalo robe coat revealing a massive Colt Walker. The could plainly see percussion caps filling all the nipples.

His fingertips were splayed around the handle of the weapon and the three men with him all averted their eyes. "Didn't mean nothing, boss," Lopez said.

"And you, Whitmore? You want out?"

"No way, Crazy Ned. I'm in for the duration. I like money, but I don't like cold. Let's rob a bank in Mexico next time."

That took the edge off the conversation, and Crazy Ned let his coat fall back into place. "Not a bad idea, scientist."

Washoe City was the county seat of Washoe County and sat along the banks of Washoe Lake. Next to Virginia City or San Francisco, Washoe City was one of the busiest places in the west. Vast amounts of timber were harvested in the Sierra Nevada to feed the mines of the fabulously rich Comstock Lode, just over the Virginia Range to the east.

The mines couldn't operate without great steam engines. They powered the hoists and other machinery needed, and there was lots of machinery. Beside fuel for the steam engines, the mines were going deeper and deeper, and the ground was not solid rock. Cave ins happened often, and vast amounts of timber were needed to hold the mountain in place while tons of ore were removed. Washoe Lake's lumber mills were the heart of the operation.

Timber was sent in flumes from the high Sierra to the lake where it was floated to large mills. From there, lumber was lashed to wagons which were drawn by mule and ox teams over Jumbo Grade to the waiting mines in Virginia City. Cash flow through the bank in Washoe City was large, as Crazy Ned Paulson knew. It was so close, he thought, he could almost smell the gold.

"Ain't none of us gonna ever be cold again with the amount of gold we gonna have bulgin' in our pokes." His eyes were wild, quickly looking at each man, the valley below, and the high Sierra, seemingly all at the same time.

He howled and yipped, laughing wildly, carrying on like the mad-man he was. "We gonna meet up with Beulah Bender tonight and she'll give us the details of how that bank operates. This time tomorrow, boys, we gonna be rich, rich, rich." The laughter, mad, wild, that Crazy Ned let loose echoed through the Virginia Range canyons, maybe even down to lake level.

Beulah Bender was often called Big B, a heavy, not very attractive working girl employed by Maude James at Big Maude's Pleasure Palace in Washoe City. Beulah was known to extract extra bucks from time to time from gentleman caller's pockets, use a shiv on those not willing to pay a fair price for her wares, and helped men like Crazy Ned Paulson get the low-down on places that needed some plundering, such as the Washoe City Bank.

Big Maude knew Paulson was coming and had her own plans. Crazy Ned Paulson wasn't the brilliant outlaw he thought he was and could be manipulated by a woman with the wiles of Big Maude James.

The bank sat on the corner directly across from Big Maude's so Big B was able to do her investigating by way of sitting in her upstairs window, allowing potential customers to view the merchandise at the same time. There was a lot of merchandise to view.

"We ain't gonna have to camp out in some damn ice field, now, are we?" Lefty Lopez asked. "Ain't gonna do that, Crazy Ned. Ain't."

"Can it, Lopez. I ain't never done you boys wrong and I ain't gonna start now. We'll spend the night at Big Maude's Pleasure Palace. I don't think I have to tell you to keep your damn mouths shut."

Big Maude was hostess to all sorts, but it was the lower levels of society she preferred doing business with, such as bank robbers, even the scum of the sort such as Little Al Tyson. She got her share of their dealings, sometimes without them knowing about it. She knew Crazy Ned was going to pull off the bank robbery; she also knew he wasn't going to leave town with the proceeds.

CHAPTER 2

BIG MAUDE'S PLEASURE PALACE WAS WARM, SMOKY, AND noisy as the four men made their way to the bar. Stale beer, spilled whiskey, and spat tobacco juice were among the lively flavors in the air. Oil lamps hung from the ceiling of the two story combination saloon, whorehouse, gambling house complex. "There's Big Maude at the end of the bar," Crazy Ned Paulson said. "Find a table, boys. I'll get a bottle and be right with you."

Paulson eased his way to Big Maude's side and nodded hello, the move returned by way of a fluttering of eyelashes. Big Maude broke away from the man she was talking to and stood next to Paulson. "Glad you made it back. Didn't believe it, though, when I got your note." she said.

Big Maude's name was Belinda James and her husband, Jake, was barman at the establishment. Big Maude owned the joint and everyone knew it, but it was Jake who was on all the paperwork since a woman couldn't own either a whore house or a saloon in Washoe County. Jake James was just a needed man to sign the papers. He did what he was told to do, didn't make or cause trouble, and smiled sweetly at his wife when commanded to do so. The working girls also knew he did his best to take advantage of them.

"What brings you back this way, Sam?"

"Gold, Big Maude, lots of gold. Those are my men at the table by the piano. Care to join us?"

"For a piece or two of the gold I'll join anyone, Sam Sampson. Even you." She gave him a big smile, and yelled at Jake. "Bring us a bottle and glasses, Jake, and make it snappy. You remember Singin' Sam don't you?"

"I remember," Jake said. He glowered at Sam Sampson. "Enjoy that bounty money did you, Sam? I didn't enjoy the three years. What brings you back? Lookin' to squeal on someone?"

Samuel Gantry Sampson, known to ex-cons as Singin' Sammy because he turned on everyone who ever worked a job with him, was also known as Crazy Ned Paulson, and from time to time as Peter Hollister. Each of his monikers carried their own personalities, their own specialties as far as breaking the law went. Each had wanted posters out with fair representations of what the man looked like.

Paulson introduced the gang to Big Maude and settled into a chair. "Gonna hit that bank in the morning, Maude. Thank you for doing some checkin' on it for us."

"You ain't hiding out here when you're done, Sam. Ain't no way. Sheriff will start his search here and you know it. Don't mix me up in this." Big Maude James's eyes were pinpoints of anger when she snarled it out. She saw that Paulson was taking the bait. "You bring trouble with you, Sam, and I ain't buying in. You're welcome to spend the night, as I've told you before, but that's all. You're out of here in the morning."

Jake James brought the bottle and glasses to the table, glared at Sampson, and went back to his duties behind the oaken plank. *Ain't no good coming from this. Maude better remember what happened to me. Dirty wild man's gonna create nothin' but trouble.*

"We're gonna need a place to get to, Maude," Sam said. "You've been here in Washoe Valley. If we can't stay here, where can we hide until things blow over?"

"With Sheriff Hansen, things ain't gonna blow over, Sam. Your best bet is to hightail it clear out of the county. Go south or east. Stay away from me."

"We are heading for San Francisco when things cool off, but need someplace to hide for a week or two. Come on, Maude, I ain't never got you in trouble."

"You sure as hell got Jake three years' hard time. He won't never forget that, Sam." She looked at this man with the single braid down his back, snow white from being burned in a barn fire when he was a youngster. "All right," she smiled, glad he fell for trap. "I got a cabin up Parker Canyon. It's got food and beds and cut wood. I've hid folks up there before. I'll draw you a map, but you better not turn on me, Sam. You better not or you'll find yourself missing parts."

———

No one paid any attention when a long, lean millworker walked away from the bar and headed out the heavy doors of the saloon. He crunched his way through old and icy snow to the telegraph office two blocks down the street.

The wire read, in part, "Positive that Samuel Gantry Sampson, aka Crazy Ned Paulson is in Washoe City, Nevada Territory. With at least four men, two of whom also are wanted. Please advise. Don't trust the local sheriff. Duffy, Deputy U.S. Marshal."

"Send this off immediately, Mr. Campbell. I'll check tomorrow for an answer."

"On its way, Duf." The wire operator looked at the message and then looked back at Duffy. "That bastard was here a couple of years ago. Tore the place up. Hope you can put him away for a long time. There are still a few around town who remember him."

Michael J. Duffy, Deputy U.S. Marshal, smiled at Campbell and walked slowly back to Big Maude's Pleasure Palace. *He sure as hell was here. Wonder what's brought him back? My guess would be the bank.*

———

"I DON'T LIKE IT, Maude. That bastard will make big trouble for us, for you." Jake James was having supper with Maude in their apartment at the top of the stairs. The working girls had their rooms down two hallways off the stairs. "First deputy to smack him and he'll tell everyone that you set him up, that you planned the robbery, that you, you, you. I know," Jake said.

"I know how he operates, Jake, but he's got something going here that might be to my liking. That bank has got lots of gold in the vault right now and he'll pull it off, sure as I'm standing here. That man knows how to rob a bank."

She sat back and smiled. "Ain't nothing wrong with us taking our share, is there?"

Jake's eyes narrowed down as the thought took hold. He got a crooked smile across his ruddy face thinking of just how much money was about to be theirs. "You've got something up that sleeve? What?"

Maude saw a lot of greed in those eyes staring at her. She had seen death in them at the table, earlier, when he was talking with Crazy Ned. She could put all that together to her benefit. Despite his size, which was considerable, Jake did what he was told when it was her doing the telling. He had spent three years in prison in California before coming to Nevada Territory and finding warmth, food, and security with Big Maude. Jake James was not a smart man. He would do what he was told, but had not had an independent thought for years.

"I'm sending them up Parker Canyon to the cabin. Let's put some of our boys together and see what we can do about it, eh? Finish your supper and head out to the ranch. You shouldn't need but three of the boys to take Sam and his boys out." Jake's eyes brightened when she said that and the smile slowly crept across his ugly face. "They don't need to know why we want those four dead, only that they'll be paid well. Don't mess up, Jake."

Jake James was a killer and this idea brought an ugly grin to his face when he got to his feet. "I'll eat later, Big Maude." She could almost feel his hatred for Singing Sammy as he left the bawdy house for the long ride to Big Maude's small cattle ranch along the south-east shore of Washoe Lake.

Now I get even. Three years I sat in that hell-hole, letting my hate build every single day. You are gonna die hard, Sam Sampson. Just as hard as hell is hot.

The men who worked the cattle were in the

bunkhouse when Jake got there. He explained without going into detail that four men had made Big Maude angry enough that she wanted them dead. "I need two of you to ride with me tomorrow. You'll be paid well for this, and Big Maude will do everything she can to protect you from the sheriff."

Two men spoke right up but the others shunned the idea. "Don't want that kind of trouble," one said. Jake told the two to meet him at the Pleasure Palace early in the morning and they would make their way to Parker Canyon. He then rode back into town and spent the night in the warmth of Big Maude's welcoming arms and legs.

CHAPTER 3

Heavy pounding on the hotel door brought Bull Morrison slowly out of a lovely dream he was enjoying. Something about fighting natives, naked Island women running about, and flagons of rum being offered regularly.

"What! Damn!" He stumbled to the door and jerked it open, forgetting he hadn't bothered to put his pants on. Slim Calhoun burst into laughter, almost pointing at the naked and very large U.S. Marshal, glaring at him through red rimmed and well hungover eyes. "What do you want?"

"Get dressed, Bull. Time to hit the road." Calhoun started to hand him the wire he just picked up, took a second look at those eyes and decided it would be best if he read it to him. "Listen. Just got this wire from Mike Duffy up in Nevada Territory," and he read the telegram. At the words, Singing Sammy Sampson, Bull Morrison came close to being sober.

"We've got him if we hurry. We can be there in three days or less." Slim Calhoun pushed his way into the hotel room, suggested the big marshal get dressed, and talked a blue streak. "How long has it been since we got a real lead on that fool, two years? Duffy isn't one to go off on a lark, either. This is what we've been waiting for Bull."

Five feet nine inches tall, 195 pounds (no fat), Bull Morrison, United States Marshal was slow getting his head around what his deputy, Slim Calhoun was saying. Morrison proudly carried a brutal and ugly scar across his face. It came from a broken bottle wielded by a man who hasn't drawn a breath since. That scar brightens with Morrison's level of anger or desire to fight. And fighting was what Bull Morrison lived for.

According to Calhoun, Bull Morrison combed his hair with his fingers and a wash rag once or twice a week, lived to fight, and his version of right and wrong wasn't always the way it's written in the law books. He came by the law the hard way, learning that the man with the badge carried a lot of weight. Scrappy little boys, arrogant because of their strength and bullying, were made to change their ways because of this one man in Bull's youth.

Bull grew up fast when the man with the badge became his stepfather, learned that good manners got him favors that bullying didn't. He never lost the desire to fight, though.

"Singin Sammy, eh? This is good news, Slim. Good news. Wonder what he's doing in Washoe City? Raiding lumber mills isn't exactly his cup of tea. Beating women, that would be, but what else would take him to Washoe City?"

"Gold, Bull. That bank's been ripe for some time. The Comstock Lode is exploding, new millionaires daily, and those mines need every board foot of timber as can be cut in the Sierra. Every inch of it passes through Washoe Valley and those mills are making as much money as the mines they serve. Crazy Ned Paulson has been a bank robber all his life. He was in Washoe City a couple of years ago. That's when we started chasing the bastard."

"Two horses and a mule, Slim. See to it. I'll see the judge and get us some money and book passage to Sacramento. Take us a day to get there and then two, maybe three days over them high mountains. Why does this always happen in the middle of damn winter?"

"I'll send a wire back to Mike Duffy, too. He's a good man. See if he can keep an eye on whatever Paulson is up to without being seen. Far as I know, no one in Washoe City knows he's a marshal. They will soon."

"Meet me at Italian Joe's on the waterfront with the animals. I could eat a gray whale right now. We'll take the night boat to Sacramento and be able to ride right out of town in the morning."

Six feet tall and 190 pounds, Slim Calhoun had longish light colored hair that tended toward being a bit wavy. He had a sly grin, and felt strongly about his partnership with Bull Morrison and the job they do. They are not alike at all, rather almost opposites, yet would defend and respect each other while joshing and bitching about each other all the time.

Slim had a wicked sense of humor, often aimed at Morrison, but also in general. The deputy marshal had been known to see humor in some awkward situations sometimes. Unlike Bull Morrison, Slim Calhoun had a deep sense of right and wrong. Those who know him well believed that might stem from early childhood when his parents were wronged and almost lost the family farm. An old-time county sheriff saved the family and young Slim wanted to be a lawman from that moment on.

Calhoun had an eye for lovely ladies and they were drawn to his good looks and naturally easy manner as well. It took a couple of hours getting the horses and mule, getting provisions for four days, and getting the animals and gear down to the waterfront. He got the animals loaded on the steamboat and found Bull Morrison at Italian Joe's, bowls of pasta, platters of pork chops, and great tureens of soup on the table.

"About time you showed up. I had a fear that I might have to eat all of this all by myself. Get everything?"

"I got everything, Bull." Slim Calhoun sat down and filled a plate. "Got the animals on board the boat and got our stuff tucked away in our cabin. What happened to your nose?"

Bull Morrison took a swipe at his nose with a napkin, looked at the blood stain, and gave a little smile at Slim. "Damn fool tried to get in line in front of me is all. Tried to stab me with a fork, Slim. Can't let something like just get passed by could I?"

"Of course not," Calhoun snickered. "Why, Bull, he could have hurt you."

"Damn right. They'll take good care of him at San Francisco General. At least the man didn't break any furniture when he fell down. Twice."

"I guess that means you aren't gonna tell me the whole story, eh? We'll dock in Sacramento sometime near sunrise, Bull, and I figure we can make at least fifty miles, maybe more tomorrow. After that we'll be in those high mountains and won't make good mileage.

Only thing to slow us down would be storms or you getting in fights with everyone we meet."

"Well, Slim old friend, as I've said so many times, it isn't me that starts them fights. People take a great dislike to me, mostly cuz I'm so damn good looking it scares 'em, and then they start pushing. You know what I mean?"

"I know what it is I see," Calhoun chuckled. "I'd like us to be in Washoe City four days from now. Don't want to lose this opportunity to put Crazy Ned Paulson away for good. He's about as slippery a man as we've had the pleasure of chasing."

"Too many years chasing him, Slim. Think Duffy will keep close eyes on him?"

"I sent him a wire saying he better. Signed your name to it."

They finished the large meal, and were about to leave Italian Joe's when Joe Stagnaro called to them. "Hey, Mister Marshal. Who's a-gonna pay for da busted platters, cups, spilled soup, eh?"

Slim automatically reached for the leather pouch he wore as a necklace. "How much damage, Joe? Be nice to us. We'll be gone for some time."

"Better for my business when you're gone. Twenty dollars."

"No, Joe, that's too much. Bull Morrison couldn't have done that much damage. I'll give you five." Joe stood still for a minute, looked at Bull, then Slim.

"Okay, five dollars and don't come back for a long time. You eat good," he smiled, "but you cost me money." He took the five-dollar gold coin and tucked it in his apron, gave Slim a smile, scowled at Bull, and headed back toward the kitchen.

"Only five dollars' damage? I'm out of shape." Bull Morrison laughed, pushing the doors open and walking into a wall of thick fog. "Love this overnight trip up the river to Sac City. Boat rocking some puts me in a deep sleep. Let's get it on, Slim Calhoun."

CHAPTER 4

WASHOE COUNTY DEPUTY SHERIFF WILSON 'BEER BELLY' Garrity was hurrying the best he could through the muddy main street of Washoe City to the sheriff's office located on the main floor of the county courthouse. "Sheriff," he said, gasping for breath after crashing through the front door. "I'm dead sure I just saw Crazy Ned Paulson having breakfast at Uncle Bob's Café. I'm sure of it."

"Yeah, well last week you saw Jack the Ripper getting a haircut and sometime last month you told me Wahkeen Murrietta was in town. Go have a cup of coffee and check on our prisoners."

Sheriff Dan Hansen hired Garrity because he was a cousin of the chairman of the county commission and the commissioner enjoyed playing little political jokes. Hansen planned to get even.

"No, Sheriff, I mean it. It was Crazy Ned and he had three other men with him."

"Who were they? Maybe the kid? Or was it Buffalo Bill? Get out of here."

Garrity's head hung low as he slipped through the back door and into the jail area. "Sheriff doesn't believe me," he said to the jailer. "I know it was Crazy Ned Paulson sitting at the table at Uncle Bob's."

"Why didn't you arrest him, then?" jailer Mockingbird Jessup said. "Ain't that what deputies are supposed to do?"

"He had three men with him. I come to get the sheriff and he don't believe me."

"Well," Mockingbird said. "Just get busy taking these slop buckets out. Sure be glad when they get the latrines dug for the jail. Can't use the courthouse facilities after John Johansen blew 'em up. Get them smelly buckets out of here."

Garrity hated this part of being a deputy sheriff but had been told by the sheriff it was a part of his job and if he wanted to wear that badge he better do a good job of it.

———

CRAZY NED PAULSON and his gang sat around a big table at Uncle Bob's Café eating stacks of hot cakes, platters of pork chops, and gallons of coffee after a night of revelry at Big Maude's Pleasure Palace.

"That Weeping Winona ain't a bad one at all," Sonny Jackson said. "By golly I was warm as toast all night."

"Just remember what it was Big Maude told us about that bank over there," Crazy Ned said. He pulled a watch from his vest and gave it a long look. "She said those doors were never late getting open, and the bank didn't have a guard or anyone walking around with guns."

He checked his watch one more time. "It's nine-thirty now and Sonny, you, me, and Lefty want to walk in those doors over there at ten sharp. Jackson, you be outside those doors with the horses. Don't be shootin' anybody unless you have to. Us inside will be doing a bit of shootin' for sure."

"I got those feed bags to stuff full of gold," Jack Whitmore said.

"Good," Crazy Ned said. "Let's walk nice and slow over to the corrals and get our horses." He looked at the three men and continued. "We've gone over this, but one more time won't hurt. If we should get separated, make for that Parker Canyon camp."

Parker Canyon ran deep into the Carson Range of the Sierra Nevada, following what was called Galena Creek that ran year around. Timber was thick and there would be deep snow this time of the year. An old cabin, built by prospectors years ago and abandoned, gave shelter and could be defended.

"We got to have this timed just right," Paulson said. "We'll come down the street from the corrals, leave the horses with Sonny, and hit those doors just as the bank opens. Let's move it."

The four men walked the half block from Uncle Bob's to the Washoe City Stables, saddled the horses, and slowly walked them back down the ice crusted muddy street to the bank building. There were few people out and about on such a cold morning, and those that were paid little attention. Drifters moving through Washoe Valley, either toward Virginia City, or

Carson City, even north to the new community of Lake's Crossing, were a common sight.

Jack Whitmore took the reins from the other horses as the men stepped down from their saddles. He convinced Sonny it was best if he kept charge of the horses. Each man had a feed sack bundled under their heavy coats and kept their heads lowered and hats pulled down, didn't look up and down the street, only paid attention when the big doors of the bank swung open. Crazy Ned Paulson led the way in followed immediately by Lefty Lopez and Sonny Jackson.

The clerk was behind the counter, the manager standing off to the side, a big smile welcoming these first customers. "Good morning, gentlemen," he said. The smile froze solid when Paulson pulled that Colt-Walker and slapped him across the side of the head. Lopez leaped the counter and smashed the clerk in the head with his six-gun before the clerk could get the vault doors shut, and Sonny stood with his shotgun pointed at the front door.

"Let's get those bags filled, boys. Sonny, shoot the first sumbitch to come through those doors. Yee haw but this is fun." Crazy Ned Paulson did a little dance, singing out yee haw all the way to the vault.

Bank manager Horace deWhitt lay on the floor, his head bleeding profusely, and watched as his vault was quickly emptied. His vision wasn't the best under ideal conditions, but he was sure he recognized the leader of the gang. It had to be Crazy Ned Paulson. Between the wild eyes, the long single braid of almost white hair, and the crazy yelling and dancing, deWhitt was positive it was Crazy Ned, back again.

Two years earlier, just as Washoe City was coming

together, just as the mills were starting up, just as the big mines in Virginia City were being organized, while the district was a part of Utah Territory, Crazy Ned and a gang of ruthless killers came through town, killing, raping, robbing. The bank manager was whipped by the man and left to die. Horace deWhitt would never forget that mad face.

Now, the district was called Nevada Territory, and talk of statehood was rampant. Washoe City was flourishing, Virginia City was awash in millionaires, and there was even talk of a railroad sometime in the future. Horace deWhitt watched as Crazy Ned and the two men with him ran from the bank, feed bags filled with gold and silver coins. The bandits didn't bother with the paper money. Who could trust that stuff?

It was the clerk who was able to get to his feet first, and as he stumbled toward the big doors to raise the alarm, Celinda O'Mally from Uncle Bob's Café walked in. She screamed, seeing deWhitt on the floor, covered in blood, and seeing the clerk staggering toward her. She looked back and wondered, *were those the same men who just had breakfast at the café?*

The screams could be heard up and down the main street and people flocked to see what the ruckus was. Four horsemen walked their mounts north, watching those around them closely. One man ran for the sheriff, and it took Dan Hansen a little time to understand what was being yelled at him. "The bank?" He looked at the man, looked around the office. "What about the bank?"

"It was robbed, Sheriff. Mr. deWhitt is murdered. There's blood everywhere. Everybody's dead."

Hansen got to his feet, wrenched himself into a buffalo robe coat, and grabbed his shotgun. "Out of my way," he said, shoving his way through the door and making his way the long block to the bank. Celinda was on her knees trying to get the blood stopped from deWhitt's head wounds.

"He's hurt bad, Sheriff. So is the clerk."

"Go get a doctor," Hansen said and kneeled down to talk with the bank manager.

CHAPTER 5

"THAT'S IMPOSSIBLE, DEWHITT," SHERIFF HANSEN SAID. He was on his haunches talking to the bank manager as the doctor worked on the man's bashed in head. "Crazy Ned Paulson hasn't been seen in this county for a couple of years. Your head ain't right from the knock it took. Couldn't possibly be Paulson."

"No man can miss what that fiend looks like, Sheriff. I seen him before, and I seen him this morning. It was Crazy Ned Paulson that robbed this bank this morning. Why are you arguing with me? Get my money back!" He was thrashing about, trying to shake a fist at the sheriff, demanding that the man do something other than argue with him.

"Take it easy, Horace," Doctor James Elroy said, easing the man back down. Sheriff Hansen stood up and walked to the big doors of the bank. *Garrity said he saw Paulson and now deWhitt says he's seen Paulson. Both can't be wrong.*

Hansen stopped half a dozen people, asking if they

saw the men leave the bank. Some remembered seeing the four horses being ridden out of town, north toward Lake's Crossing, and Hansen huffed his way to the office.

"Garrity!" he hollered out a couple of times before the deputy came out from the jail.

"Right here, Sheriff," he said. "Buckets all swamped."

"Good, I'm gonna gather up a posse. Go saddle your horse and meet me here in ten minutes. We got a hard ride in front of us. Go now."

Garrity hot-footed it to the stables and saddled his buckskin dun. *Wonder what this is all about? Heard an uproar, I did, but for the sheriff to put a posse together? That's most unusual.* Garrity couldn't remember the last time one was called up. Sheriff Dan Hansen wasn't one to go off chasing banditos. He was more likely to send Garrity or maybe even Mockingbird rather than go himself.

Garrity mounted the dun and rode up in front of the sheriff's office where Hansen sat his red roan, surrounded by three men he collected from The Timbers Saloon. "Word is the four men rode north toward Lake's Crossing. They ain't gonna go that far, I'm sure, so watch out on the sides of the roadway for four horses moving off. Let's ride boys."

"Who are we chasing, Sheriff?" Terry Bovary asked, trying his best not to slur his words.

"What happened?" Deputy Garrity asked.

"The Ned Paulson gang just robbed the bank, that's who we're chasing," Hansen said.

"Crazy Ned Paulson? I told you I seen them men this morning," Garrity said. "I knew I was right."

"You were right. Now shut up and watch for riders moving off the main road."

The sheriff was in front with Terry Bovary and Johnny Snyder riding right behind. Deputy Garrity fell back to bring up the rear. Washoe City was about twenty miles south of Lake's Crossing, but the sheriff was sure the gang would get off the main road and head either for Virginia City to the east, or into the Sierra Nevada to the west.

They weren't half a mile and Garrity called out, pointing at obvious signs of horses leaving the main road and taking a road almost due north toward a defile that lead them to Galena Creek and Parker Canyon. "Don't seem right, but these are the prints from four horses and that's what we're looking for," Sheriff Hansen said. Nobody mentioned that the sheriff and his posse rode right by the prints and it was Deputy Garrity who saw them.

"Garrity, you lead. Stay on their trail. Don't lose that trail." The sheriff now was the one hanging back letting his deputy ride into the trouble that might lie in front of the posse. Garrity was filled with pride, understanding that he now had the lead, could be the one first to capture these murdering bank robbers.

"We'll get 'em, Sheriff," he yelled back. The trail was as easy to follow as if painted signs were left for them. Fresh snow on a seldom used single track that led deep into the forests of the Carson Range. The trampled snow left by four horses were now trampled by Sheriff Hansen and his posse.

———

"How much further, Crazy Ned?" Lefty Lopez asked. "This snow's getting deeper every foot we go higher into this forest."

"Big Maude said it was about five miles into the trees, Lefty. Just keep leading us in. She said it was just off this trail and could be seen easily. We gotta cross a creek before we get to it."

The four were riding single file through less than a foot of snow that half an hour before was a couple of inches of snow. The road was definitely going up into the heavy timber of the Sierra Nevada, and the cold was going down as fast as they were going up.

Lefty led them across a ridge and the path led down through a large stand of aspen to a creek. As he rode down toward the water the shelf of ice broke off and the horse plunged in, catching itself in about three feet of icy water. Lefty Lopez was an excellent rider and rode the bucking and plunging horse to the other side of the creek.

Gonna be a mess getting out. Gonna be an ice shelf on this side, too. He chuckled a bit thinking it would have been better if Crazy Ned was leading. *He'd be in the water, flailing about, calling old Lefty Lopez to save him.* The snickers weren't heard by those following.

Lefty's horse pawed at the snow bank that draped over the creek's edge, finally knocking it back to the iced bank, and climbed out of the cold water. The others followed, griping and cursing the whole way across the stream and climbing out. "Let's keep it going, Lopez," Crazy Ned called out as his horse made the climb out of the creek. "Can't be too much further."

Left Lopez led the gang into a grove of tall pines about an hour later, pulling his horse up in front of a log cabin. There was a corral behind the house with storm stalls backed up to a hillside. The cabin featured two chimneys, one near the front and one close to the side in the back.

"Ain't no sign anyone's been here," Lopez called out. "No horses in the corrals. No smoke in the chimneys."

———

"HEAR THAT?" Jake and the ranch hands huddled by the window watching Crazy Ned lead his gang in. "Good thing we hid those horses, eh?" He had a wicked sneer on his face watching the group. *I been waitin' for this a long time, Singing Sammy. Come beggin' for a job, let you ride with me on a bank job, and what do you do? Send me to prison for three long damn years. Here's to you, you rat bastard.*

There was cut and split wood stacked on a covered porch, out of the snow, and the front door of the cabin was standing open. "Our new home for a short time, boys," Crazy Ned Paulson said as he and the gang, still fifty yards or so from the cabin, rode slowly in. "Let's get our stuff inside and get fires lit. Got to be below zero out here."

Those were the last words uttered by Crazy Ned Paulson, also known as Samuel Gantry Sampson. Rifle fire erupted from the cabin, two large caliber round balls blew through Crazy Ned's chest, throwing him back and off his horse.

Two rounds hit Sonny Jackson, one in the chest, killing him, and one in the leg that went all the way through and into his horse, killing him, too. Lefty Lopez dove to the ground and rolled through the snow to get behind a large pine and Jack Whitmore did about the same. The two men were behind different trees about fifteen yards or so apart.

"What the hell?" Lopez cried out. "We've been set up. Big Maude James sent us here to die."

Whitmore had his heavy Colt Walker out and cocked but couldn't see anything through the open door of the cabin. "Don't know how many there are, Lefty, but they've had time to reload. Got any ideas?"

"Yeah," Lopez snarled. "Kill those bastards and then Big Maude." He was quiet for a minute. *Those horses are standing quiet, each one carrying a heavy feed sack filled with gold and silver. We gotta kill those bastards in that cabin. Got to.*

"If I fire a round or two in that door, can you move forward? Got to kill those bastards."

"Let's give it a try," Whitmore yelled back.

Lefty pulled his old Colt, made sure each nipple had a cap, cocked it, and put two rounds through the open door. At the first shot, Jack Whitmore made a plunge for a tree about ten feet closer to the cabin, and was killed by two shots from the cabin.

They are at the windows not the door. Lopez was in a spot now and he knew it. He wasn't the type of man to panic, he'd been in tight spots before, but this one had to be the worst of them all. *I don't even know how many there are. Nobody's yelling out, nobody's talking at all. Gotta save myself but sure would like to save all that gold, too.*

Gold has a way of making men do strange things, and the amount of gold and silver coins strapped on those horses was making Lefty think wrong. He had more interest in keeping the gold for himself than he did for saving his life. Since he had no idea who was in that cabin the idea of trading the gold for his life never entered his mind. Would they have made the trade? Lefty would never know.

He slowly let himself down into a sitting position and studied the situation. The horses were all together, pawing snow out of the way and grazing on grass, each with a feed sack filled with gold and silver. *Can I get anywhere near at least one of them?* They were twenty-five yards or more away across open ground. Not a tree or piece of brush between him and safety.

Hell, even if I got there, they'd kill the horse to get me. I gotta make contact with whoever's in that cabin. Gotta know who is there and how many. I wonder if Maude James sent Jake to ambush us?

The day had started at ten in the morning when the bank opened and Lefty Lopez was well aware that in just a short time it would be dusk. *Dark is my friend. I can get one of those horses and be out of here.*

The cabin sat in a hollow of Parker Canyon on the east slope of the mighty Sierra Nevada, and the sun dipped behind those high ridges early in the afternoon. But, it didn't get past dusk for hours. He was in the shadow of high mountains and it wasn't long before he saw smoke coming from the two chimneys.

As soon as the sun dipped behind those high peaks the cold settled in and Lefty Lopez was sure that even if those bastards, all warm and cozy in the cabin, didn't kill him the cold would. *Can't wait. I gotta make a move now. Now, while I still can.*

He didn't have to think about it too long and hollered out, "You, in the cabin, want to talk some?"

"Got nothing to talk about," a voice answered.

Was that Jake James? I'll kill Big Maude if I get out of

this. "I got a lot of gold out here. Let me go and it's all yours."

"You ain't got shit, Lefty. That gold is already ours. We'll just sit here by the fire and let you freeze to death. Got hot coffee, got a pot of beans boiling. Life is good in the cabin, Lefty."

"I ain't never done you wrong, Jake. It was Crazy Ned talked on you. I wasn't even around in those days. Let me have a horse and I'll just ride off."

"Can't do that, Lefty. You know too much." Jake was right and Lefty knew it. He knew that Maude knew about the bank heist. He knew that Jake killed his friends and had the gold. He also knew he was a dead man.

"Can't we make some kind of a deal, Jake? I ain't like Singing Sammy. I ain't never talked on a man. I'll just ride out and you'll never hear from me again."

"Sorry about that, Lopez. Been screwed once. Never again."

It was much darker now and Lopez looked around, saw that he could move back toward a stand of trees without those in the cabin seeing him. *Better let it get darker than this. Another few minutes.* When he had a hard time even seeing the horses, he eased away from the tree and moved slowly back keeping the tree between him and the cabin. He was twenty feet or so back when a voice behind him said, "Sorry, Lefty," and the bullet ground its way through the bandit's heart.

CHAPTER 6

"IT'S GETTIN' DARK, SHERIFF. HOW MUCH FURTHER WE got to go?" Beer Belly Garrity was still leading the posse, the sun had dipped below the high Sierra ridge, and the temperature was falling fast. Terry Bovary and Johnny Snyder, the other posse members echoed Garrity's question.

"We go until we find them," Sheriff Dan Hansen snarled. *Ain't any real men out there anymore. Not like when I was younger.* "We cross a creek up ahead and there's an old hunting shack not far along. We'll stop there for the night."

Garrity wanted to say something more but didn't. He wanted to ask, "What if that's where the gang is? We shouldn't just ride in like we own the place." But he didn't. Garrity was one of those men who simply flowed with the tide, rarely if ever questioning what happening around him, much less why.

Sheriff Dan Hansen was a domineering type man, demanded this and that, often just on a whim, such as when he made it department policy that the deputy clean the honey pots every morning. He had been elected sheriff because he bought more drinks at The Timbers Saloon than his opposition and that was because his family had money, not Dan Hansen.

The creek crossing was made easier because the Crazy Ned Paulson gang, coming through earlier, knocked the ice shelves down from the creek banks. It was just a short time after crossing the creek that Garrity saw lights from the cabin and could smell smoke from the fires. "Just ahead of us, Sheriff, and the gang is already there."

Hansen rode up to the front fast, and took in the situation. Dusk was now night, but with light from the cabin window he could see several horses in a corral. More than four. Did that mean the gang was more than four? Or did they just have extra horses? He had been told by several in town that there were four men robbed the bank.

"Must be six or seven horses in that corral," Garrity said. "They got help, Sheriff. Only the four of us. What do we do?"

"Four men robbed the bank so these men brought extra horses, planning on a long run," the sheriff said. "There are four of us, four of them." He looked at Garrity and the other two. "It may be dark, but it's early evening. Now's the time to hit 'em hard, Garrity. You and Terry Bovary circle around to the back of that cabin and when I start shooting, you two start as well."

Garrity wasn't pleased with that idea but knew he couldn't argue either. Those extra fifty pounds he carried weren't going to help him plow through all that snow to get around the cabin.

Sheriff Hansen continued. "Johnny Snyder and I

will ease our way as close to the cabin as we can get. I'll call 'em out and if they don't come out, we'll start shooting into the cabin. When you hear us shooting, then you start."

Bovary looked at Garrity then at the sheriff. "Ever thought that maybe this ain't the gang? This is part of a big ranch, Sheriff. This might be some cowboys in their line camp. Wouldn't want to be killing some innocent cowboys."

"Then, when I call 'em out they best come out runnin' eh?" Hansen could see an opportunity here, make a big name for himself, get himself reelected and then make a run for governor. *This Nevada Territory is gonna be a state before long. Now's the right time to make a big name for myself. Killing the Crazy Ned Paulson gang is gonna be my ticket to the governor's mansion for sure.* He almost said it right out. "Governor of the State of Nevada." *That has a nice ring to it.*

––––––

"MOVEMENT OUT THERE, JAKE," one of the men yelled out. "Looks like four men on horses. Gotta be the sheriff and his posse. Good thing we got those bodies hid. Looks like they're gonna ride right up to the door."

"We kill the sheriff we're gonna bring a lot of people wanting answers, boys. We done a good job on Singing Sammy and company. Big Maude's gonna pay you boys well, so let's not let anybody get away. Got to be quick and clean. What do you see, Bobby?" Jake remembered the one thing that sent him to prison. A witness. Singing Sammy, not just a partner in crime, but a witness who told the sheriff everything. "We can't afford to leave any witnesses."

"Two of 'em trying to stay in the trees and come around to the back, looks like."

"You and Minton get out there and surprise them with a knife or two. Don't shoot 'em." Big Jake James looked around at the three hands he brought up from Big Maude's ranch. "That damn sheriff would turn and race back to town if he heard a gunshot. Nobody knows that we're out here. Only the four of us. The sheriff thinks we are the Crazy Ned Paulson gang. He'll die thinking that."

Jake thought Big Maude had it planned well. Somebody would be sure to come out this way checking on why the sheriff didn't return, would find the bodies of the Paulson gang and the bodies of the sheriff and his gang, and think they killed each other. *Big Maude was right again.*

In the meantime, all that gold and silver from the bank would be in Big Maude's little safe at the Palace. Jake had other thoughts moving through his head as well. *Gotta keep these three jaspers from talking, too. Maude ain't gonna want to give them a lot of gold. That fat bitch won't want to give them nothing.* He had to hold in a snicker, coughed a bit, and motioned for the back door.

"Get out there and take those two out. Me and Julius will take care of the sheriff." He motioned for Julius to take the window to the left of the front door and he'd take the other. Julius Maynard grinned as he moved to the window and eased down, his rifle poised and ready.

"Look at that, would you?" Maynard said. "Sheriff's riding right up to the door like he had been an invited guest."

"He's mine," Jake said. "Make your shot, Julius. Can't let one of 'em run away." Jake saw the sheriff and Johnny Snyder ride up to within ten yards of the cabin. Hansen pulled his rifle, saw Snyder pull his, and Jake eased his trigger back. Sheriff Dan Hansen was flung back off his horse and before Johnny Snyder could even raise his rifle, a bullet put an end to his life as well.

"Good shooting, Mr. Maynard. Let's see how Bobby Jones and Elroy Minton are doing out back." Jake James stood up and as Julius Maynard walked past him toward the back door, a large skinning knife was plunged through his back and into his heart. Maynard was dead in seconds and Jake eased his revolver from its holster and walked to the back door.

It took just a second for him to see that Bobby Jones and Elroy Minton had disposed of Beer Belly Garrity and Terry Bovary. Jake stepped out the door and waved the two over. As they turned toward him, he fired twice, killing both with shots through the heart. *Ain't never gonna let a partner live again. Ever.*

For the next hour Jake James moved bodies into the cabin and just left them strewn about. *It would be fun to be here when somebody finds this mess. I got to get those horses loaded with all this gold and silver and get back to Washoe City.* He had to laugh looking around. *Ain't nobody but me knows how all this happened and I sure as hell ain't saying nothing. This will put a smile on Big Maude's fat face.* It was Big Maude's plan and Jake never took that into consideration. Jake not only had a partner, it was her plan, and yes, Jake, she could get you sent back to prison.

He led a pack train of all the horses back into Washoe City late that night. If he was seen, no one spoke about it. He got the horses tended to at the Pleasure Palace corrals, and one at a time brought the heavy sacks of loot into the whorehouse. He was strong as an ox, just couldn't think. Why didn't Jake James just ride north to Lake's Crossing and then east to Denver or west to San Francisco? Why would never be answered.

———

"IT WENT EVEN BETTER than I planned, Maude. Crazy Ned's gang and the sheriff and his posse, gone away. I didn't like having to kill the boys from the ranch but we couldn't have three witnesses walking around."

"No, we couldn't," Big Maude said. She gave him a little look out of the side of her eyes. *No, Jake we certainly can't be leaving witnesses.* "You did right, Jake. Let's get all this gold in the vault and see to it that those feed sacks disappear, too. Sure as hell somebody would recognize them. It's all anyone in town can talk about, how the bank was robbed. Horace deWhitt ain't dead but he's close. Doc says he'll live."

The four sacks which would normally hold fifty pounds of chicken feed each, held hundreds of pounds of gold and silver coins. Thousands of dollars. Big Maude hid a smile, thinking that only she and Jake knew where all those dollars were. *Only me and Jake,* she thought. *I wonder if that might be changed?* "There are thousands of people in this vast territory called Nevada, Jake, and we're the only ones to know where this gold and silver is."

"It's a good feeling, isn't it? You gonna count it?" Jake's mind was on gold, lots of gold, not on partnerships.

"Hell no," Big Maude laughed. "Somebody at the bank will tell one of those reporters from the *Territorial Enterprise* how much was stolen, and unless you lost some coming back into town, I'll know how much is there."

They had a good laugh, Maude poured a couple of glasses of fine whiskey, and they saluted each other. "I'm about the richest bitch you've ever had between the sheets, Jake, and I'm ready for a good maulin'." She shut the heavy doors to the vault, spun the dial, and gave Jake James an evil look. "Let's go big boy, and don't let me down."

CHAPTER 7

MIKE DUFFY WALKED INTO UNCLE BOB'S CAFÉ NOT LONG after Bob got the place open, and Celinda O'Mally walked him to a table near a window. "Gonna be another cold day," she said. "Bob's got pork chops and gravy, hot biscuits, and gallons of coffee to get you started."

Her smile was delicious, Duffy thought, looking into deep green eyes, shaded some by wisps of blondish hair coming across her forehead. *Damn shame I can feel all these years I've been enjoying. She wouldn't give me the time of day right now, but it weren't that many years ago she'da throwed herself at my kind. My kind,* he thought again. *What is my kind? Not afraid of nothing. Fight anybody, anytime, anywhere. Ceptin' maybe not this morning. Is it I'm gettin' tired? Or is it I'm gettin' old?* "Good mornin', Darlin'."

He chuckled to himself and let his eyes wander from the top of her head to her small feet and enjoyed every inch of what he saw. "Not that many years ago, young lady, I'd want you for breakfast." He smiled and was surprised to get a smile right back at him.

"You ain't that old, Buster. Don't seem like the kind of man to give up easy."

Celinda O'Mally was voluptuous in every meaning of the word. "Sounds like a good way to start the day," she said. He offered a wide smile, wanted to reach out and pat her attractive little bottom, and caught himself in time.

Instead, he destroyed the moment. "What time does the telegraph office open?"

She just looked at him and if he had been quick he'd have seen just a tinge of sadness in her eyes. "Sometime around eight or nine, I think. Ain't never needed to know before." Her little laugh was almost a tinkle and she danced away from the table toward the kitchen. Michael Duffy watched her all the way. *That was a nice message she just sent my way.* It was another message he was expecting, a wire from Bull Morrison telling what action, if any, he should take regarding the Crazy Ned Paulson gang. He had a hard time kicking Celinda out of his thoughts but after all these years carrying that deputy marshal's badge, he knew work had to come first.

By God we had 'em right here in town. There's four of 'em so Bull most likely will want me to just keep an eye on the situation until he and Slim make it over the Sierra.

His thoughts were interrupted when Mockingbird Jessup, the county jailer walked in, shaking snow and ice from his cape. "Anyone seen the sheriff?" He looked at Celinda, at Duffy, at the two men sitting at the counter, and everyone shook their heads.

"Strange," Mockingbird said, and started out the door. Duffy called out to him to come over.

Duffy pulled his badge from a vest pocket and showed it to the jailer. "I'm United States Deputy Marshal Michael Duffy. Is there a problem?"

Jessup sat down quickly and gave Duffy a long look. "Seen you around town, didn't know you was a marshal. Yeah, I think there might be a problem. Sheriff put together a posse after that bank robbery yesterday and he ain't come back. He and that fool deputy Garrity left out with Terry Bovary and Johnny Snyder and ain't none of 'em come back."

"Maybe they ain't caught the gang yet," Duffy said, trying to ease Mockingbird's anxiety. "Sometimes a chase takes more than a day."

"Well, maybe for you marshals, but not for Sheriff Hansen. He ain't missed a home cooked meal in years. He'd a come home when the sun went down." Mockingbird Jessup laughed right out at his little joke.

"Any idea of which way the gang lit out?"

Jessup looked around, trying to remember. "Yeah, I think I do know. He said something about Parker Canyon, that he would lead the posse toward Parker Canyon. You go north up the creek and follow the canyon west. Another creek comes out of that canyon and joins the one you'd be following. Nasty crossing a mile or so up the canyon creek."

"Want to take a ride? Seems as though you might be the law in the county right now."

"Cain't do that, much as I'd like to, Marshal. Got three no good drunks in the jail. Judge won't see them until tomorrow."

Duffy chuckled softly, looking at the skinny old man

who limped along using an oak staff for balance. "Could use a good man like you, Jessup, but your duty at the jail must come first.

"Was Garrity the only deputy? No one else in the department?"

"Nope, just the sheriff, Wilson Garrity, and me. I better get back, gotta keep the jail warm for those yahoos." He looked at Duffy. "What should I say if someone comes looking for the sheriff?"

"That he's out chasing the bank robbers and you don't know when he'll be back." He had to chuckle again watching the old man lurch his way out of the café. Celinda brought him his breakfast and gave him a wonderful smile and another full cup of coffee.

"Enjoy your breakfast. A marshal, eh? You look like a real bruiser. Maybe we will have breakfast together sometime." She giggled and danced back away from a hand reaching out.

"I'm planning on it," Duffy said. *Back to work, old man. She will be fun. I'll check on the wire first and then it might not be a bad idea to load up and see if I can find the sheriff's trail. This ain't the way Crazy Ned Paulson normally runs off. I'd think he'd head south and then over the Carson Road to California.*

He could see the telegraph office across and down the street some, and had an extra cup of coffee waiting for it to open. It was a quick walk through blowing snow and ice. The clock inside said eight fifteen but the thermometer hung on the porch post registered ten degrees. "Man could freeze just stopping to blow his nose," he muttered walking into the tiny office.

"Morning," he said. "Names Duffy, Michael Duffy. Got a wire for me?"

"Right here Marshal. Looks like you got them stirred up down in San Fran."

"Thanks," Duffy said, scowling some at the clerk, but understanding that of course he knew what the wire said seeing as how he was the one who received it. *Just don't like other people knowing my business.* He read the short note on the way to the stables.

Keep an eye on the gang until he and Bull get here, eh? Well, it's too late for that. I'll see what the sheriff has found out and try to keep that jailer advised as to where I might be found. The wire said that Bull Morrison and Slim Calhoun would be coming and should be in Washoe City in four or five days. *I should know something by the time they get here.*

———

"MORNIN'," Duffy said, walking into the livery. The smithy was standing as close to his fire as he could dare get. He gave Duffy a smile and made room for the deputy. "Did you happen to see the four men who robbed the bank yesterday morning? That is, which way they might have ridden off?"

"Sure," he said. "Like I told the sheriff, they started out on the north road to Lake's Crossing but then veered off onto the road that leads up toward Parker Canyon. Thought it strange at the time. Ain't nothing up there but good hunting. Fine herd of mule deer up that canyon every year."

"And the sheriff went that way, too?"

"Sure did," the smithy said. "That's something strange, too, if you know anything about Sheriff Dan Hansen. I don't think the man has ever spent one single night in a bedroll. He's always back home in time for supper, and in this weather, for him to still be out on the chase, well, sir, it just ain't logical."

"I need to rent a good pack mule and put together a kit for at least two, maybe three days. I'll go round up supplies and be back shortly," Duffy said.

"Why would you want to even get involved? That's why we elect them fellers."

Duffy laughed and pulled his badge out. "I'm one of them fellers, just not elected."

The smithy chuckled watching Mike Duffy walk off back to town. Duffy was back, quickly, with a supply of food, his bedroll and extra blankets. He had it packed and was ready to ride in less than an hour. "Anyone come looking for me, tell 'em I'm up Parker Canyon and they should follow. Give 'em good directions. The one with the scar across his face is a mean dog of a man but he is a marshal, so be nice."

"I'm always nice to the law," the smithy said, hid a slightly veiled smile, spat some tobacco juice, and waved Duffy off.

CHAPTER 8

THE WIND HAD LET UP CONSIDERABLY AS MICHAEL DUFFY made the turn from the north road onto the trail leading toward Parker Canyon. Snow continued to fall, big, cold, flakes that hid most of the countryside from view, as if riding through a heavy fog. The trail led through rolling hills populated with Piñon pine, Juniper, sometimes called stunted cedar, and sage, little of which he could see.

These kinds of rides can have two effects on the rider—either to dull the senses or allow him to open his mind and let thoughts flow like creek water over smooth rocks. Duffy was letting his mind wander and those little adventures had a lot to do with Crazy Ned Paulson but little to do with Sheriff Dan Hansen.

No matter the name he used, Crazy Ned Paulson was a killer. A demented, sadistic, killer. Duffy was well aware of the man's career and knew that if what he had heard from Mockingbird and the smithy that Hansen was not up to taking Paulson into custody. Wasn't up to killing the man, either. *The sheriff and his posse are in more danger than he's ever known.*

Through the occasional breaks in the storm he could see the massive western face of the Carson Range of the Sierra Nevada. Slide Mountain, soaring ten thousand feet into the sky and its twin, Mount Rose even higher to the north. Parker Canyon trail would wind its way, eventually, to wide and beautiful meadows that were between eight and nine thousand feet.

"Damn fine country these boys decided to be criminals in," he muttered. "Would have been better if they had picked El Paso. Warmer for sure." He had to chuckle at the thought. Duffy had been chasing the bad boys since he was eighteen years old. "Been doing this for more than twenty years. Love seeing all this beautiful country. Shame it has to be defiled by fools."

Riding through open country in the middle of an early-winter storm gives a man plenty of room to open the old storage box called memory and Duffy wasn't going to miss out on any.

Here I was standing at the bar in some run down cantina on the Mexican side of the river, across from El Paso when Felipe come runnin' in forcing a wire on me. I knew it meant I had to up and leave this old West Texas town and I tried to shoo that brat off, but he won and here I am half froze in the wilds of Nevada Territory chasin' a ghost. Call him what you want, Crazy Ned Paulson, Sammy Sampson, hell, even Peter Hollister, the only time I ever saw the gent was right here in Washoe City and now I'm chasin' him. Well, I hope I'm chasin' him.

Thoughts of other chases clouded his mind some because they had always been along the Mexican border. "I've done as much marshalling in Mexico as I have in Texas," he said right out. "That's true, horse. Ain't supposed to, you know that, but when them jingle footed outlaws cross the river, I just follow right along. Bring 'em back dead, they can't tell anyone where they got themselves all shot up, now, can they?"

It was a lively discussion as he made the crossing of Galena Creek where the trail turned due west, straight up a wonderfully wide canyon that he could see would narrow considerably in just a few miles. "Ain't never wanted to be a farmer or run cattle, but if a man felt that way, this would be the country he'd want to run in. Got water and grass, got open country and so much to look at. If I didn't love El Paso so much I might want to live here."

Ice dripping down his neck from his hat brim changed his mind immediately. "Kind of a rash thought, horse. We won't be living here."

Piñon forests gave way immediately to tall ponderosa and other pines, aspen groves, and as he gained altitude, some cedar, fir, and spruce. The cabin was just off to his right and he saw a trail that led to it. With so much fresh snow, Duffy was not able to see any prints on the trail and he saw no smoke coming from a rock chimney.

If the sheriff or Crazy Ned Paulson made it this far there sure ain't any sign of 'em. I better check that cabin anyway. Damn fool sheriff might be froze to death in there. The snickers would have been heard several yards off as Duffy made the slow ride to the cabin. Some of the snow around the front door had been disturbed and he grabbed his new rolling block rifle from its scabbard as he stepped down from the saddle.

He tied the horse and mule off and stepped onto the

porch. The front door was pulled but not all the way to, and he slowly pushed it open with the barrel of his rifle, waited a second or two, and stepped into the large room, that rifle fully at the ready.

"My god almighty." The breath was almost knocked from the long-time deputy marshal as he took in the grisly sight of bodies strewn about, frozen solid in all kinds of different poses. Ams and legs not just alongside the bodies. "These have just been thrown about in here. Not killed where they lie. What the hell have I found?" He was having a hard time taking it all in, making sense of a senseless situation. *Somebody did this. A fiend. Is he still around? Too much new snow hiding what I need to know.*

He walked to the fireplace and found the ashes were cold. The same with the wood stove in what he supposed was the kitchen. "That bank was robbed yesterday morning. That means all of this happened last night sometime. I saw no tracks because of all this fresh snow we're getting." He looked around the room and started counting, quit at seven and moved to get a fire started first.

Figure out how many dead people we have here then see if I can identify any of them. I gotta get back to Washoe City and send a wire off to Virginia City and to San Francisco. Glad Bull Morrison is coming, I'm gonna need more than just help with this mess.

With the Paulson gang, the sheriff and his deputies, and the ranch help that Big Jake brought, there were eleven bodies strewn about the cabin's main room. Duffy got some paper and a pencil from his saddle bag and drew a picture of the living room and where each body was located, then moved the bodies back outside so they would remain frozen.

The drawing noted which bodies were the sheriff and his deputy, highlighted Crazy Ned Paulson, and Duffy recognized Lefty Lopez and Sonny Jackson. He didn't know the others.

"All my years under the weight of this horrible old badge and I ain't never seen nothing like this," he muttered, stepping back in the saddle. "Damn me, but it's gonna be past sundown before I get back. Ain't no reason to stay out here, though. Got nobody to talk to here," he chuckled, giving his horse a gentle nudge. "Let's go, big boy."

———

Duffy dropped his packs off at the livery, turned the mule over to the smithy without saying anything about what he found, and slipped his horse in a stall. *Best check the telegraph office first and get those wires sent off.* He remembered that Virginia City was in Storey County so that wire went to the Storey County Sheriff, and his wire to San Francisco went to the Pacific Division Marshal.

He took the long walk from the telegraph office to the jail. "Old Mockingbird ain't gonna like what I've got to tell him. Sure hope Bull and Slim get here quick." He found the office nice and warm with a pot of coffee boiling on top of the pot-belly stove.

"Didn't expect you back for a day or two, Marshal." Mockingbird Jessup was at the sheriff's desk, his feet up, and a tin cup of coffee in hand. "Find our sheriff did you?"

"I found him but you ain't gonna like what I'm about

to tell you." The tone of his voice and glare in his eyes told Mockingbird it wasn't good news. The jailer got up and pulled a chair over next to the stove.

"Set yourself and give me the bad news."

It took almost half an hour to tell the whole story, and Jessup sat next to the stove, his mouth open, never saying a word until Duffy wrapped it up. "You're going to have to get with the county coroner and the undertaker and get those bodies brought back to town. It's best if we try to keep this as low-key as possible, but with a dead sheriff and deputy, and dead bank robbers all found together, there's gonna be some wild stories floating about."

Duffy didn't say anything about the one thing that bothered him all the way back to town. Where was the money from the bank robbery? Duffy couldn't find a farthing despite almost tearing the place apart. Somebody knew that Crazy Ned Paulson was running to that cabin and lay in wait, killing the gang and stealing the loot.

But, Duffy wondered, what about the sheriff and his posse? Did Dan Hansen just ride into an ambush? Was the sheriff in cahoots with Crazy Ned? How much of all of this was planned and by whom? "Brilliant," Duffy said right out.

"You mean the ambush?" Mockingbird looked at the marshal. "You ain't said nothing about the loot, Marshal. Where's the money?"

"Damned if I know," Duffy laughed. "Never found a dime, Mockingbird. Somebody's got it all. Somebody we don't know."

"Those that don't much care for old Dan Hansen, and there's plenty of 'em, are gonna have the time of their life," Jessup laughed. "Didn't find any of the bank's resources, did you?" Duffy chuckled and wagged his head no and Jessup continued. "Do you think the sheriff was involved with Crazy Ned Paulson?"

"Some will, you can bet. There's obviously someone we don't know about, eh?" Duffy got up slowly and looked at the jailer. "Don't you be spreading that kind of talk, Jessup. You're the sheriff now and the talk can get out of hand." Duffy had to get back to being the marshal, the all business marshal.

"A marshal and his deputy should be riding in tomorrow but you need to get to work getting those bodies back into town. Can't just leave 'em lay out there." Duffy didn't even want to think about coyotes, wolves, and mountain lions. "There's a few I didn't recognize. Try to get all of them officially identified before Bull Morrison and Slim Calhoun get here."

He reached in his pocket and pulled the drawing out. "This is how I found them. I'll leave this with you but when Bull and Slim get here we'll probably want to see it."

Mockingbird Jessup nodded and poured another cup of coffee. "Silas Pokriots is the undertaker and has a good sized wagon. He and I will go out with a wagon first thing after I feed our drunk friends back there in the cells. It looks like I'm the law around here unless you want the job."

"It's all yours, Jessup. I've got enough to worry about right now."

Duffy took a walk along the icy boardwalk of the main street in Washoe City. Looking out south, he could see lights reflected off the ice and water of Washoe Lake and could hear great steam engines pounding, driving the mills that were reducing high Sierra timber to useable lumber for the mines. Money was being made, life was going on.

Steamboats brought the raw logs, cut from the mountainsides around Lake Tahoe to the east shore where they were dragged to the ridge tops and sent wildly down great flumes to splash into Washoe Lake, then rafted to the mills. Once in a while one or two logs would go rogue and tear up the flumes but nothing slowed the mills from turning out useable lumber for the mines of the Comstock. Those mines had a voracious hunger for timber as did the steam engines that drove the hoists and pumps all day every day.

In the history of the North American continent, there had never been a richer lode of silver and gold, and millionaires by the gross were being created almost daily. While in Dakota Territory, a dollar was a fair amount of money, in Virginia City it was a hundred-dollar bank note that was used to light a cigar.

To be in the lumber business brought as much riches as being in the mining business on the Comstock. More than one of the mills was owned by mines up in those rich mountains.

Duffy turned into the Timbers Saloon and found a spot along the long bar, called for a bottle and a glass of beer, and opened the wire from Slim Calhoun. *So, they left Hangtown. Should be here tomorrow. What a mess they're riding into. Somebody has all that bank loot and that somebody is close enough to this town to let the sheriff walk right up to him, close enough to know about that cabin, and close enough to know where the bank robbers were going. Or, was that somebody a fifth member of the gang?* Duffy smiled at the barman, mumbled his thanks, and flipped a coin out. "I got questions. You got answers?"

"Sure. Two and two is four. How's that one?"

Duffy laughed and took his first long drink of cold beer. "That's the one I wanted." The barman chuckled and walked off down the bar. "I can't even begin to think of where to start," Duffy mumbled. *Who are the big people in town? Big Maude James seems to have a lot of pull at the courthouse. The sheriff did have. Who owns the major timber interests? Check on them.*

He poured his second glass of whiskey and drank half of it before finishing his beer. "It's time for a big steak dinner," he muttered, slowly pushing away from the bar. "Been one long day." Duffy had been wearing a badge for many years, had investigated many crimes that involved dead people, but the vision of all those frozen corpses in that cabin was still with him and would be for a long time.

How could something like that develop? How many people, other than the dead ones, are involved in this monster of a crime? All that fresh snow ruined the original scene and Duffy couldn't imagine just how many people might have been there considering how many dead ones were left. *Ain't gonna let it ruin my supper.*

Next door to the saloon was the Sugar Pine dinner house, and Duffy could smell venison roasting on open coals as he walked through the doors. Not quite the elegance of the dining parlors high on the Comstock, but top of the line in Washoe City, the Sugar Pine featured tables covered in linen, goblets for water, and silver utensils. Elegant Victorian lamps hung from the ceiling and some wall sconces, too, were lit. The floors were covered in fine wool carpet, and many of those seated were dressed for the occasion.

Ain't gonna find a bowl of El Paso chili in here. I'll eat as much elk as they'll serve me but I could handle a good Mexican supper right now. Chilies and meat, more chilies and cheese, and some fine Mexican music to ease the tempers. What the hell am I doing in this iced in country?

It was a dining room designed to make one feel warm and welcome. There were all the signs of the frontier, such as deer, elk, antelope, and bear heads along the walls near the bar area, stuffed and mounted salmon and trout, quail, ducks, and geese, too. Tinges of Victorian elegance mixed with the rough and tough frontier. Duffy felt the weight of the day slowly dissipate.

"Evening. Just one," Duffy said, doffing his heavy coat and hat. "And half a buffalo roasted nice and rare, if you please."

The waiter chuckled at Duffy's way of talking and led him to a table for two. "Think there's room on that table for what I want to eat?"

"I'm sure we'll make it work, Marshal. Word around town is that you went hunting for the sheriff who it seems might be lost up in the hills."

"Well, son, he ain't lost. Just not in his office at this moment." Duffy wondered how this gentleman would even know that he had been tracking the sheriff. "Let's start with a bowl of soup for four, and then work on a few elk steaks, eh?"

Cocky little bastard seems to know what's going on around town, maybe I can squeeze some answers out of him.

The waiter leaned down just a bit and in a lowered voice, and without pointing, said, "The gentleman in the red plaid wool shirt is James Osborne, the owner of the second largest lumber mill on the lake. He'd like a word with you, if you don't mind."

Duffy spotted the man, tall, broad shoulders and thick neck. "Ask him to join me." *I need to know considerably more about this waiter.*

Osborne walked over to the table, a bottle of the best whiskey the house had to offer and a glass for the marshal in hand. Duffy started to stand to welcome the man and was waved off. "No, no, Marshal, please, stay comfortable. We have a considerable lot to talk about. Those men who robbed the bank got away with a great deal of my money. Any chance of getting it back?"

Osborne sat down and poured drinks for the two of them. "Difficult question to answer, Mr. Osborne. You said your money. How's that?"

"Well, I suppose the correct thing to say is my company has a lot of money moving through that bank, including a payroll that's scheduled in two days." The man wore mutton chops that seemed to have a life of their own, was probably near fifty, had a weathered but open and friendly face. Duffy imagined he would be demanding of his employees but also worked to take care of them as well.

"I hope that bank is well insured because I doubt we'll have Crazy Ned Paulson and the money in hand in two days. How many lumber mills are there?"

"My mill provides timber and specialty cut lumber for a combine of several mines. The other mill, slightly larger than mine, provides for John Mackay and his silver barons. Neither of us is ever quite caught up," he chuckled. "Can you tell me what you've learned so far about the bank robbery? I'd like to keep my men informed."

"I'm expecting two marshals in tomorrow, Mr. Osborne. I can tell you right now that we won't have recovered any of the money in the next two days. What I'd like, though, is to sit down with you and those two coming, and get a better handle on some of the people in Washoe City. Crazy Ned Paulson had that job well planned and he wasn't in town long enough to do that kind of planning."

"You're saying he had help from someone locally? That's really not amazing." The questioning look on Osborne's face told Duffy that the man had considered that question. It also told Duffy the man was probably not involved.

"Someone or some," Duffy said. "I'll have many more answers tomorrow if I could come by the mill."

"You'd be more than welcome. What do you know about Big Maude? She's got her hands in almost everything that's illegal around Washoe City." He quickly wrote out directions, poured another drink for Duffy, and left the table, taking his bottle with him.

Careful with his money, Duffy snickered. *Local people are involved, that I can bet the ranch on, but it's going to take some work to weed them out. Glad Bull Morrison and Slim Calhoun will be here tomorrow.* He let his mind wander over the question of Big Maude James. *So the fat madam is a part of the criminal side of town, eh? That certainly isn't unusual.*

Elk steaks, still sizzling on a pewter plate, were brought to the table and the thoughts of bank robbers, dead sheriffs, and raging snow storms vanished into thin air. Fried potatoes, roasted carrots, and a carafe of red wine filled the table to overflowing. *I might be here 'till sunrise but I'll not leave a shred on my plate,* Duffy said to himself.

He caught the waiter's attention. "You seem well connected around here. What can you tell me about Big Maude James?"

"Well, I can tell you this, Marshal. According to more than one person who was there last night, Crazy Ned Paulson and the men riding with him, spent the night at Big Maude's Pleasure Palace. I heard that Big Maude and Crazy Ned were old friends."

"You are full of good tales, eh? Well, thank you for that." Duffy left wondering about that. Big Maude married to Jake James, recently out of prison, being good friends with Crazy Ned Paulson who just robbed the bank and was now dead, dead, dead. *And all that money is missing. Heavy bags full of gold coins, missing.*

CHAPTER 9

HIS BELLY WAS FILLED TO OVERFLOWING, THE STORM HAD abated, and Deputy Marshal Michael Duffy made his way back to his hotel in a happier and warmer mood. *I now know a couple of timber industry names and found out a few things about a few of the Washoe City nabobs. This will help the investigation along nicely. Hope Morrison and Calhoun get here early tomorrow.*

Bull Morrison and Slim Calhoun were just fifteen miles away in the territorial capitol of Carson City, finishing their supper at the St. Charles Hotel. "We'll leave out early, Slim. It's an easy ride to Washoe City. Looking forward to seeing old Duffy again. He's older than us, skinny as a rail and tougher than a bull moose on the prod. You'll like him."

"I've heard stories," Slim said. "I've heard that he's the man in the El Paso district. What's he doing here? We're a long ways from Texas."

Bull Morrison chuckled and speared a chunk of left-over elk roast before trying to answer. "He's been on the trail of Sam Sampson for a couple of years. The man changes names as often as we do socks, Slim. Word got out that Sampson might be in Nevada Territory and the service sent Duffy to find him. That's why we're here."

"It would have been better if Singing Sammy had been holed up in El Paso. At least it would have been warmer. It had to be ten below when we left Strawberry. Let's take a bottle to one of those tables by the fireplace and talk about this Sammy Sampson fool."

"No, Slim, let's take a bottle and sit at one of those tables by the fireplace and drink what's in the bottle. Talking about that fool would just get me riled, and it's been two full days since I been riled."

Slim Calhoun laughed right out, motioned for the bartender to bring a bottle, and settled in. The fireplace was a big rock affair with what looked like half a cord of wood burning brightly, warming the almost elegant saloon. The St. Charles Hotel was a three story affair housing the saloon, a small café, the large dining room, and a barber shop. The upper stories were home to the hotel rooms.

The St. Charles was the leading hotel in Carson City, sat almost across the street from the capitol building. Members of the territorial legislature stayed there, visiting dignitaries, government officials, and mining nabobs made the hotel central to their business.

A gentleman played the piano while most of the customers were at the bar drinking. As the evening progressed, the gaming tables would fill and more than likely at least one fight would get underway. Just across the street was the new territorial capitol building and it had been quite a fight between Virginia City and Carson City over which would be the territorial capital.

"Duffy tell you how much money was stolen from

that bank?" Calhoun asked. "I'd think there would be quite a bit."

"Well over twenty-five thousand," Bull said. "Mostly gold coins and some silver. Both the banker and his clerk were severely beaten but haven't died—yet. That's a bundle of coins to take care of. Crazy Ned Paulson had three men with him according to the wire. It would take four to handle that much money in coins."

"Hard to hide," Slim said. "I notice you call Sampson Crazy Ned more often than Singing Sammy. Any reason why?"

Bull took a long drink of whiskey. "Singing Sammy has never killed anyone, Slim, but when he's on a rampage, he's Crazy Ned Paulson and he's a butcher. Thinking of the banker and his clerk, it was Paulson who robbed that bank. Interestingly, each personality that Sampson assumes is unique. The man is mad as they come, you know. What's that figure of speech you like?"

"Crazy as a loon," Slim chuckled. "Good at robbing a bank, though."

————

IT WAS a quick breakfast and an easy fifteen mile ride to Washoe City, along the banks of the big lake, now covered in a heavy blanket of icy fog. From high on a ridge they could hear the deep thumping of steam engines on the plain below. The road north wound its way up and over a high bench that was locally called Lakeview.

There was no wind and the fresh snow glistened in the early morning light when they rode up and over the ridge, out of the fog. The Virginia Range to their east was home to the Comstock Lode, and the massive Sierra Nevada, to their west, was home to so many stories and myths, legends and truths. And timber.

"Do they get spring and summer in this country?" Bull Morrison was wearing a wool shirt over his long johns, a sweater over that, and was wrapped in a heavy buffalo robe, cinched tight with harness leather. "Enough ice in that lake to keep more than ten years' worth of beer cold."

Slim Calhoun led them along the banks of the lake, through high stands of sage and stunted cedar, moving in and out of the fog. One trail led around the west side, into the foothills covered in heavy pine forests, locally called Franktown, while another branch covered the east side of the lake. They were following the east side trail.

Michael Duffy's hotel was in Washoe City at the far north end of the lake, and they found the man in a conversation with the barman. "Hello, you old codger," Bull said, giving the deputy marshal a big shove as he stepped to the bar. "Can't catch Crazy Ned standing at the bar."

"Already catched," Duffy said. Slim Calhoun noticed that there was no smile coming from the marshal. Duffy continued. "Dead as last year's news. Let's find a table cuz you ain't gonna believe a word I say."

———

JAMES OSBORN WAS at his desk looking at the pained face of Bull Morrison. That deep red scar that careened across his scowling face seemed to have a life of its own.

Osborn knew the man was a U.S. Marshal but was astute enough to recognize he would be most dangerous in any physical altercation. He almost snickered, thinking how glad he was that he was on the right side of the law.

Also at the meeting in Osborn's mill company office was Slim Calhoun and Mike Duffy. Morrison just outlined what was found at the Parker Canyon cabin. "What you just described is more than horrendous, Marshal. I've never heard of anything more gruesome in all my life."

"I've carried a badge for a long time, sir, and I've never run into anything like this." Bull Morrison looked around to Slim and Duffy. "We're more than sure that whoever was behind those killings not only has the bank's money but is also a well-known local person."

"I can't imagine anyone being that blood thirsty."

"Sweet old ladies kill almost as often as mean and filthy men," Duffy said. "Crazy Ned Paulson wasn't in town long enough to have known where to go to get away. He would be more apt to run for Lake's Crossing, to get away on the emigrant trails, not to a cabin deep in the Carson Range of the Sierra Nevada."

"Good point," Osborn said. "Does anyone know whose cabin that is? I've hunted the Parker Canyon many times, seen the cabin and never given it a thought."

"It's been noted that Maude James may own it. She has a ranch tucked in the forest east of the lake as well. Two of the bodies found at the cabin were men who worked for her at the ranch." Slim Calhoun said. "We haven't got it all figured out, but right now, she has to be our number one person."

"She's involved in everything illegal," Osborn said, his eyes alive with mirth. "Can't picture the fat old broad killing off that many people. Her husband Jake is a foul-mouthed, lazy, card sharp. Wouldn't think he'd have the guts for such a job."

"Are there others in the community who are known criminals? This was almost planned. Somebody knew what Crazy Ned was up to and aimed him to that cabin," Bull said. "Was it the sheriff behind the entire thing? I doubt it but you'll hear a lot of people suggesting it. Why did Paulson run to that cabin? Why did the sheriff go to that cabin?"

"Easy, Bull. You're getting riled," Slim Calhoun said." He smiled and looked at Osborn. "Don't want him getting riled."

"I need a drink," Bull Morrison said. "Let's hit the saloon and have a long talk."

Duffy had to smile and led the bunch out of Osborn's office. "We'll keep you informed, Osborn. You do the same for us if you hear anything."

"You bet I will," Osborn said. "There's one man who it's believed runs a small gang. He worked for me for a short time. His gang of ruffians rob travelers, do small time robberies, and have been known to kidnap young girls. He's Albert Tyson but calls himself Little Al. He's at least twice my size," Osborn said.

He sat back down and watched through a large window as the three men made their way across the mill yard to their horses. *I can't imagine what kind of fight that Morrison fellow was in to get a scar like that.*

CHAPTER 10

"I'M TELLING YOU, IT'S AVAILABLE," JAKE SAID. HE WAS AT Little Al's, a stink hole of a saloon along the south shore of Washoe Lake, well outside the village of Washoe City. The saloon was a long cabin with one door, one window, dirt floor, and a slab of pine held on top of two barrels for a bar.

A trail branched off the main road around the east side of the lake, wide enough for one horse that connected to Jumbo Grade, the wagon road from Washoe City to Virginia City. There were some that called it the outlaw trail, including the Storey County Sheriff. Little Al Tyson's saloon was at the trail head.

'Little Al' Tyson was a monster of a man, tall, heavy, and meaner than cat-shit. He had been a woodcutter, lumber mill worker, and mule-skinner in past lives. Oh, and a bank robber, sneak thief, and murderer, too.

"I only need you and another good man, and we could pull this off."

Little Al Tyson rocked back on his heels and eyed Jake James as if looking into the open mouth of a rattler.

"You're a creep, Jake. A no-good, back-stabbing creep, but if you're even coming close to telling me the truth, you need to keep talking. Big Maude was behind all those dead men? Make me believe it."

Jake spent the next half hour convincing Little Al that Big Maude James had set up Crazy Ned Paulson and that it was Jake himself done the killing. "I know where the money is, Al. I know how to get the money but I need you and one other to make it work."

Jake had been fuming for two days following the killing. Maude had taken every single coin, to the lowest in value, and tucked them in her vault, not offering a single one to her so-called husband. Now, with some help from the likes of Little Al, he would have most of those coins and Big Maude would have none.

"I got no reason on this rocky earth to believe you, Jake," Tyson said. He shook his head, scowled at Big Jake, and laughed right out. "But I may. Damn me, but I might just believe you." Little Al walked down the length of the bar, found the bottle of good stuff instead of what he had poured Jake, and poured for the two of them. "You just said you don't know the combination to that big safe of hers and then said you know how to get it open. Better not be screwing with me, Jake." He picked up a double bladed ax and with just one hand on the handle, swung it down on a log next to the waiting rock fireplace, cleaving it in half.

Jake looked at the man and almost shivered. Little Al's hands were huge. Long fingers, gnarled knuckles, even tattoos up and down massive arms stemming from his days on the Mississippi. Little Al was wearing the top to long johns, the sleeves missing, and his hairy shoulders rippled with every move the man made. Jake could almost see him tear a man's head right off the shoulders.

"Maude ain't one for pain, Little Al. Getting the combination is the least of our worries."

"You're a real bastard, Jake, but I do like gold. You turn on me like you did those cowboys and I'll roast your liver and eat your heart, too. You make a move on Little Al and it'll be your last."

Jake felt the electric jolt of reality roar up and down his spine, thinking of that monster getting his hands on him. "We'll be partners, Little Al. I won't do you dirt. I like gold, just as much you do."

They continued drinking, slowly letting a plan come into focus. They had not decided on a third man but Jake was certain he would be needed. Mostly because there was so much gold that would be moved along with whatever other money Maude might have in that big vault. After all, her whorehouse was the busiest one in Washoe City. What to do with Maude's remains were not in the discussion.

———

MIKE DUFFY LED Bull and Slim into The Timbers, a saloon and gambling parlor almost across from the courthouse. There was little to brag about, Bull Morrison thought, looking at plank walls, filthy hanging oil lamps, and a bar with bits of dirt, crust, stains from a year or so ago, and a barman who might have died yesterday.

It was the aroma of stale beer, spilled whiskey, and kerosene burning in shaded lamps that brought a smile to the marshal's lips. "I like this place," Bull said. "Lots of personality." Duffy and Slim Calhoun just kept walking toward the bar. "My kind of place." There were some mill workers lined up at the bar and Bull Morrison shoved his way between two of them, knocking a beer glass over.

"What the hell you think you're doing?" one of the workers bawled. "Knocked my damn beer over."

"Then move over when a man wants room at the bar," Morrison said. He shoved the man again, spilling another beer in the process. "Think you own this shit hole? Give me room, damn it."

The mill worker had shoulders as wide as Bull's, stood about an inch taller than the big marshal, but lacked in the desire to fight. Bull Morrison lived to fight. He glared at Bull who in turn pushed him back again. "Give me room," Bull snarled.

"Snarly bastard, aren't you?" the man said, and pushed back hard. The fight was on and it was a one round affair. Bull howled with delight and lit into the man, knocking him all the way across the floor with two solid punches, one to his nose and one to his midsection. The mill worker was done and his friends grabbed him and hustled him out the door, calling Bull several nasty names.

"Oh, no," Slim Calhoun almost whispered. Duffy didn't even try to hide a grin, and all hell broke loose at the bar. The man with the spilled beer was out the door but the excitement wasn't over.

There were five mill workers enjoying their beer when it started. Bull watched the two leave the saloon, they were out of the fight immediately and turned on the third when the terrible blast from a shotgun broke up the melee. "One more punch gets thrown and the other barrel goes into the man throwin' it."

The barman stood back from his side of the bar holding a double barrel ten gauge shot gun still smoking from the first blast. He was rotund, bald, probably fifty years old, and his eyes told everyone that he would do as he said he would. The long barrel of that goose gun swung slowly back and forth among the angry men lined up at the bar and each and every one of them tried to stand back a step or two.

"Now, you," and the gun was pointed directly at Bull Morrison. "Get out and take your friends with you. Don't be comin' back, neither. Don't need your kind in here."

"Come on, Smitty," Mike Duffy said to the barman. "It was an accident. Won't happen again."

"I know you're a marshal, Duffy, and you've been drinking in here for a few days, but I don't need troublemakers like him," and he pointed the shotgun right at Bull Morrison, "in my place."

Duffy took a careful step up to the bar. "These two men with me are marshals, too, Smitty. Won't be no more trouble."

Bull wiped some blood from a cut lip and slowly uncurled his fists, the knuckles of his right hand bleeding freely. "Let's have some beer," he said. "I'm buying."

It took the barman a second or two to slowly lower the shotgun and Slim was quick to note that he reloaded the one barrel before setting the big gun down. There was no smile as he poured drinks for the three marshals, but a smile did come forward when Bull nodded at the mill workers.

"Them, too, Smitty. Hell's bells, boys, that was fun, eh? Didn't break nothing, I guess." The smile was lopsided but genuine and the mill boys chuckled some and toasted each other with full flagons of cold beer. A couple of them seemed glad that the fracas was called off. The idea of going up against that intimidating monster was more than they wanted.

Slim took a couple of quick looks around The Timbers and knew that Smitty used that shotgun often to break up fights. He could see the effects of more than one blast in the ceiling. "Let's take a table," he said. "We need to have a better grasp of just what's going on. The bank robbery is one thing, but all those bodies make it quite another."

Bull was thinking of the man whose beer he had spilled first. He didn't seem to have a fight in him and those with him didn't either. "If I was looking to hire an outlaw for a big job, where would I start?" He looked at the men at the bar and motioned for Slim and Duffy to go on ahead and take a table.

Bull walked up to the group and singled one out to ask the question. "Well, you gotta understand, I ain't no outlaw," the man stammered.

"Oh, hell, I could tell that right off. Outlaw would have gone for a weapon. But, let's say I wanted to hire a mean one, where would I look?"

The mill workers looked back and forth at each other, and one piped up. "Probably try at Little Al's down on the south shore. Lotta activity down that way that don't have a lot to do with drinking."

Several chuckles were heard and Bull clapped the man on the shoulder and headed for Slim's table. "Sometimes you gotta work at it to get the good information," he said with a crooked and still bleeding smile. He looked at Duffy. "Does the name Little Al's Saloon mean anything to you?"

"Heard it mentioned a time or two. Al Tyson is a gorilla of a man, big as a brown bear, and just about as mean. Rumors have it that the criminal element in the valley use his saloon as a meeting hall."

Slim chuckled at the thought, almost seeing someone holding a meeting of outlaws. "You're almost too well known in this town already, Duffy, but me and Bull might get away with a little visit to Little Al's."

"After this rumble in here, you two will be even more well-known than I am. I'd say pay a visit this evening before the word spreads who you are."

"I think I'll go alone," Bull said. "Got the fresh marks on my face. Slim, find out what you can about this Big Maude's place. Heard the name a couple of times. We'll meet back up in the morning. Duffy, make the rounds as you've been doing and keep your ears open. Somebody knows all about those killings and the bank robbery."

"Hard to hide that much gold," Duffy said.

"Not if you have your own vault," Slim said.

"Or hidey hole," Bull put in. He drank up and walked out the door, mounted up, and rode out of town to the south.

"He did it again, Duffy. Ordered drinks for the house and left me to pay for 'em." Duffy joined Calhoun in a good laugh. "I've been riding with that man for several years and the fact he rarely gets beat up, almost never loses one of these fights amazes the hell out of me."

"Do you have any ideas on those killings?" Duffy asked. "So far, my only thoughts are that whoever did the shooting was well known to the men getting shot. Nobody shot back."

"That and the fact the shooter only took enough of the animals to carry all the money from the bank. Great feed bags full of gold and silver." Slim cocked his head, took a sip of whiskey, and stared at the ceiling for a moment. "Something missing? Who got to that cabin first? Was the sheriff waiting for Paulson? Did Paulson get there first?"

"You've got all the right questions, Slim, and I ain't got a single answer. I do have one question, though. Assuming for a minute that Paulson seemed to know where to go, who told him about that cabin? He hadn't been anywhere near Washoe City for several years yet knew about this lonely cabin up in the mountains? Make you wonder, don't it?"

"Yup." Slim kept staring into the fire. "We know that the gang spent the night before the robbery at Big Maude's. They told us that at the café. They had breakfast at the café before they robbed the bank. Think Big Maude's involved?"

CHAPTER 11

IT WAS EARLY AFTERNOON AS BULL MORRISON RODE south from Washoe City. He passed by two large mills, right down on the water's edge. The roadway was back up a rise, and once past the mills, the roadway dipped almost down to lakeside. Heavy brush lined both sides of the wide road and he continually kicked up quail and cottontail rabbits.

The Virginia Range foothills started abruptly about half a mile back from the water and Bull noticed that the further south he rode the closer the hills pressed in. At the south end of the lake, the hills were at the water's edge.

On this afternoon Bull was riding through calm air, bitter cold, but no wind and no snowflakes driven into his face. He settled deep in the saddle and just let his horse follow the trail. *Got to figure this out. Somebody in Washoe City was close enough to Crazy Ned Paulson to set him up for the killing. How did the sheriff get himself involved? Who rode off from that forest cabin with feed bags full of gold and silver? Why were those cowboys involved?* He knew he had all the right questions. "Who has the answers?" He said it right out loud and only his horse heard him.

It was about an eight mile ride and Morrison passed two ranches that started at lakeside in the valley and worked their way up into the rugged and rocky Virginia Range. Several groups of deer were grazing openly in the pastures. The trail turned down right to the water's edge and Morrison was riding on sand, even letting his horse ride out a yard or two into the lake, breaking ice and splashing some water.

If he liked catfish and venison, a man could live comfortably right along here. Despite the distance from the village, the continual thumping of great steam engines, the heartbeat of industry could be heard. He saw small steam boats on the lake putting together a raft of logs to be towed or pushed to one of the mills. *Might be a bit noisy, though.*

Bull Morrison surprised himself thinking about someone living along lakeside. Was he thinking of himself? He'd been carrying that heavy badge for so many years, had more scars than most of the men fighting that big war back east. *Ain't time to retire. Wouldn't know what to do with my time if I did. I like to eat beef but don't want to raise the damn things, don't know how to build anything, can't pound iron into something nice.*

What would a man of Bull's character do after the life of a marshal? Most who were able to leave the service alive found themselves as county sheriff or town marshal. Some worked security for express companies or banks. Would a man like Bull Morrison be able to sit on the porch and watch the world go by? Not in this lifetime.

He wasn't willing to come right out and say it, but he did understand that the only thing he knew how to do really well was fight, arrest people, or shoot them. Bull chuckled softly. "Well, horse, best listen to me now. Gotta find a little dinky town full of mean, angry outlaws and proclaim myself sheriff and spend my retirement cleaning up the mess."

The trail moved back up onto a ledge between the start of the mountain and lakeside, and into heavier brush. Piñon pine, cottonwood, and scrawny scrub cedar lined the road. He saw a horse trail lead off up into the mountains on his left just as Little Al's Saloon came into view on his right.

It was a thrown together shack that may have been a hay barn at one time, or maybe a three-sided storm stall for a pony. The roof resembled cedar shakes miss-cut, misplaced, and rotting while the board and batten walls were well aged.

That must be what Duffy called the outlaw's trail. Sure ain't a trail for heavy wagons. He said it branched off that main road and came down through the rocks right up to Little Al's.

Smoke from the chimney and two horses tethered outside an open door told him the place was open and Bull Morrison rode up to a rail and tied off. He could smell the saloon before he made it to the door, gave a slight tug to his holstered forty-five, to make for a quick draw if needed, and walked into Little Al's.

Smoke and foul air was his greeting. It was dark, just one or two lamps fighting for enough oxygen to keep lit, didn't offer much light, and Bull made his way to the plank bar. A rock fireplace dominated one wall and was blazing.

Bull took in a deep breath when he spotted the barman. That barman was the biggest feature of the saloon and Bull was impressed. There were two men, outfitted as ranch hands standing at the bar, and one older man sitting in a chair by the fireplace seemingly half asleep.

It was noteworthy to the marshal that there was just the one door and just one window. *Might get exciting if lead starts flying.*

"Howdy. How about a beer and a shot," Bull said, standing down from the two ranch hands.

"How about showing some gold," Little Al said, not moving from his spot at the end of the bar.

Man learned about customer service in some prison, I think, Bull thought. He dropped a couple of silver dollars on the plank and Al Tyson slowly got to his feet. Morrison let out a little breath realizing the man was almost seven feet tall and had to weigh hundreds of pounds. Little Al's long heavy fingers wrapped around an earthen jug of whiskey and poured a hefty shot before dipping beer from an open keg. Bull didn't see an iota of foam and wondered how the man could stay in business offering such crap.

"Ain't seen you before," Tyson said, picking up both coins.

Won't see me again, either, Bull thought. "Ain't been here before. Heading for Carson City and had a great thirst seeing your place. That trail over there lead to the Comstock?"

"Couldn't tell you. Ain't never been on it," Little Al lied. "What's your business in Carson?"

"Cattle," Bull said. "Be buying for the packing plant at Brown's Crossing. Comstock needs far more beef than the ranches around Lake's Crossing can provide."

He saw Little Al give a quick look at the two ranch hands, the slightest smile dancing in his eyes, and dipped another stale beer from the keg. "Must take a bit of gold to be buying beef for the Comstock," Tyson said. "You plan to drive those beeves to Brown's Crossing?"

"No, they've got their own hands for that. I'm just the buyer." Bull wanted to smile seeing the response from both Little Al and the two men at the bar. *Somebody's gonna be following me out of here. Good opportunity for me to learn something.*

"That was sure a mess of trouble north of Washoe City," Bull said. "I heard there were fifteen bodies all laid out near Parker Canyon. Thousands of dollars of gold from the bank robbery missing, too. Be nice to find that, eh?"

"Heard about that," Little Al said. "Yup, be nice to find all that gold. Damn fool sheriff getting mixed up with Crazy Ned, wasn't his best move."

"I guess so," Bull said. "Might stop by here on the way back to Lake's Crossing. See you," he said, and walked out. He rode off at a trot, only far enough that he was out of sight of the place and ducked quickly into some heavy brush, just off the roadway.

I'm figuring five minutes or less, he snickered, sitting his horse behind some scrub cedar and tall sage.

He was wrong. Three minutes later he heard two horses coming down the road and watched the two ranch hands ride on by. They knew this was the only road so missed seeing his prints lead off into the brush. Bull quickly followed them until they started up toward Lakeview, and kicked his horse up into a solid lope.

"Well, here we are again, eh, boys?" he hollered out from behind as he rode up on the two. "Had to relieve myself of that beer back there when you passed on by. Headin' to Carson are you?"

The one on the right swung his horse around, and grabbing for a side arm, found himself flung backwards, right off the tail end of his horse, carrying a heavy forty-five slug deep in his chest. He hit the mud and ice, flopped around a bit, and died. Bull Morrison's big revolver was still smoking when it was cocked and aimed at the other man.

"Step down nice and slow, there, mister. Your friend might want company and I'm ready to send him some."

"You ain't got no call doin' that."

"Really?" Bull snorted a couple of times, his way of laughing. "Gosh, I'm so sorry." He stepped down from his tall roan and swung a mighty left into the second cowboy's face, knocking the man to the ground. Morrison watched as the man's hand crept close to his sidearm.

"Do it and die," Bull said, ever so softly. "Pull that iron nice and slow and give it a mighty heave down toward the lake. Good boy. Now, pull your partner's gun and do the same thing." He watched the man slowly pull the dead man's gun and heave it deep into the brush, his revolver never wavering, pointed directly at the man's head.

"You ain't dressed as a highway man, more as a

cowboy. You do side jobs for Little Al? Take out a rider alone on the road? How about murder? You involved in those killings?" Bull hammered questions at the man, never giving him time to answer. "Well?" The fist seemed to come out of nowhere and the cowboy was on his back again.

"Best come up with some answers, mister. I ain't good at waitin' around."

"You're crazy," the cowboy said. Bull stepped right up to him and drove his fist down into the man's face.

"Crazy as a loon," Bull snickered, using Slim Calhoun's thought. "Talk to me or die cuz it don't matter which to me." The revolver was menacing, the man was fearsome, and the cowboy spent a full minute talking about Little Al, giving out names and places.

"Did you know the cowboys whose bodies were found with Crazy Ned and the sheriff?"

"Sure. They worked for Big Maude. Her ranch is on the other side of Lakeview from here. They do for Jake James what Kimble and I do for Little Al."

Bull knew he just learned something important. Little Al ran a gang of thieves, highwaymen, and killers, and apparently so did Big Maude's husband. *Big Maude's name keeps cropping up. Time to pay her a visit. Is it her husband running the gang or is it Big Maude?*

"You'll find the horses a couple of miles up the trail. Ever see me again, your best bet is run like the devil himself because I will kill you on sight."

Bull was in the saddle, held the reins of the other horses, and rode off at a trot toward Lakeview. He waved at the cowboy who was screaming a load of cuss words at him. *He's lucky I left him with his pants and boots.*

Bull rode around the south end of the lake and up

into the lower foothills of the Carson Range before turning north. The ride back to Washoe City was through deep grass, obvious even through the deep snow. The open range was back some from the western shore, and the long ride gave him lots of time for thinking.

Bull Morrison rode through some fine grazing land and not being a cattleman, it didn't represent anything of particular interest. Having spent an hour wondering what he might do if he gave up the badge, riding through lush pastures should have sparked an idea. Bull Morrison would not make it as a retired man. He was a lawman from toenails to hairline, and his mind was on murder, not fat cattle.

Paulson's gang emptied the bank's vault and someone stole that money. Whoever did that would need a large vault as well. Any one of those saloons might have a large vault. Any one of the whorehouses might have a large vault. Can't just go barging in and demand we have a look-see. He was laughing gently as he made his way through some dense timber, back a mile or so from the lake's edge.

He looked out across the lake and up the mountains on its far side. "Thousands of people mining millions in silver and gold on the other side of that mountain. Thousands of people down here making it easier for them, and at least one of them killed all those people and is holding thousands of dollars of blood money. Somebody wrote a story about a needle in a hay stack." The irony of his situation brought more gentle laughter from the marshal.

The ride was an easy one despite considerable amounts of snow and ice on the ground. The Sierra Nevada rose almost straight up from the little valley, and the timber that covered the mountains was coveted by those who owned the pounding steam engines. The beauty of the valley, of the two mountain ranges that surrounded the valley, and even the lake itself, was lost on U.S. Marshal Bull Morrison. He only had thoughts of murder for his riding companion.

CHAPTER 12

"Listen to me, Little Al. The man is a United States Marshal. There are three of 'em in town. We gotta lay low for a short time. That money ain't going nowhere."

"It better not, Jake, or you'll find yourself dead in hell. Man comes into my saloon, makes a big lie, kills one of my men, and you tell me he's a lawman? That he's chasing that bank loot? I'm wondering, Jake, just who's lying?"

Al Tyson had a way of flexing his arm and shoulder muscles, an intimidation that had Jake ready to piss his pants. Jake had thousands of dollars tucked away in Big Maude's vault and needed this man, this huge ape who was ready to tear Jake's head off if he thought he was being lied to.

"It ain't me, Al. Smitty at The Timbers saw their badges. They're here to find the loot and we gotta wait for them to give up."

"I ain't good on waiting, Jake. Need to rid ourselves of them, get the money, and leave Nevada Territory."

Jake saw murder in Little Al's eyes, saw ripples of

muscles up and down those massive arms, saw death very close at hand. At the same time Jake knew that Al Tyson was right. Now would be a good time to grab that loot and get out of Nevada Territory. "What to do with those marshals?" Jake asked.

"Same thing you did with the sheriff, Jake. Let someone tell them there might be something going on down here at my place and me and the boys will take care of 'em. Ain't never killed me a genuine U.S. Marshal. That ugly bastard is all mine, Jake. He's mine."

Little Al had been given a story by the ugly one, Bull Morrison, and he fell for the story. Fell hard enough that one of his men was killed and another humiliated. Little Al's fingers flexed in anticipation of gripping that ugly bastard's neck, squeezing it to the point of blood vessels bursting, eye balls popping, and a U.S. Marshal dying, a grotesque look on his face. Little Al smiled at the thought.

"I'll have my men ready, Jake. You do your part, but if you turn on me, I'll hang you by your manhood from that cottonwood tree in front of Maude's place."

"I don't turn on partners," Jake said, heading out the door. Little Al didn't catch the lie. Wasn't Jake's wife, Big Maude, his partner?

———

BULL, Slim, and Duffy were having breakfast at Uncle Bob's Bakery, not seeing the beautiful lady serving them, not seeing great flakes of snow being hammered into the window near their table, not even tasting the thick bear steaks they were feasting on. The only thoughts were on Big Maude and Little Al and the bodies brought to town from Parker Canyon.

"Must be they ain't got a lot of hogs in this country," Duffy said. "Had some bear ribs the first night here. Took three washings to get all the grease out of my beard."

"Best bear I've ever had is Grizzly hump. Not as good as buffalo hump but better than this," Bull said. He didn't have a pleasant look but was literally wolfing his steak. "Man's gotta eat," he chuckled.

"Let's get serious now, gents," Slim said. "Have you visited Maude's place, Duffy? The word is out who we are so if we visit it will have to be a pleasure visit not a business call," Slim Calhoun said.

"She runs a small gang, not as well put together as Little Al's," Duffy said. "What Bull told us about Al Tyson's gang, Maude's is below second class. Jake is her husband, but in name only. She had to have a husband. Washoe County won't give a woman a license for a saloon or whorehouse. She uses him for strong-arm stuff, mostly, and maybe a hit on somebody who has done her wrong. Small time outlaw, that's Jake James."

"Unless he's behind those killings," Bull said. His initial thoughts of Maude's husband running a gang were partially answered. For two days Bull had gone back and forth, trying to put Jake as the Parker Canyon killer, and then making it Little Al Tyson. "What if Jake wasn't involved in the Parker Canyon killings. What if it was Little Al's people?"

"If it was Little Al's gang he would be in San Francisco or Salt Lake City by now," Slim said. "The way you described the man he doesn't give me the impression of being a homebody. With all that money, he would have run and fast." He looked around the table and the other two were nodding but Bull's face told Slim he wasn't really sure of that.

Calhoun smiled. "Unless Jake and Little Al were working for Big Maude." He saw the other two draw in deep breaths, look at each other, and then put big questioning eyes on Calhoun.

"You got anything more on that thought?" Bull asked. "Think we could get a couple more of these steaks. I'm hungry as a bear."

Celinda O'Mally's tinkle of a laugh caught everyone's attention. "How long you been standing there, girl?" Bull whirled in his chair, grabbing Celinda's wrist. "How long?"

"Easy there, Bull. She just walked up," Slim said. "Don't get riled. It's too early in the morning for that."

Bull slowly released the girl and she stepped back quickly, rubbing her wrist. He put the fear of death in the girl. "I didn't mean nothing," she whimpered. "Thought it was funny you eating bear steaks saying you were hungry as a bear. That's all."

Duffy laughed right out. "She's right. That is funny."

Bull harrumphed, looked down at the floor for a moment, and then into the girl's eyes, making her step back another couple of feet. "I'm sorry, ma'am. Just a little worked up by what it is us three are working on. Don't be coming up behind me like that."

"Bull, why don't you and me take a wander over to Big Maude's place and see what we can learn?" Mike Duffy had the feeling he'd better get the big man out of the café, and in a hurry.

"Good idea. Let's go," Bull said and stood up,

grabbed his coat and hat, and made for the door that fast.

He did it again. I pay. Slim Calhoun chuckled. Celinda O'Mally handed him the bill and he gave her a big smile. "Bull didn't mean anything, Celinda. It kind of goes with being a marshal. Usually someone coming up behind you means injury or death."

"He's scary. I sure won't never do nothing like that again. Are you going to find out who killed the sheriff and all those men? My goodness, I almost walked into that bank while it was being robbed. My heart ain't gonna take much more of this." That little tinkle of a laugh had a charm to it, Slim thought. It hadn't caught anyone's attention that Bull didn't stick around for that second helping of greasy bear steaks.

"You been in Washoe City for some time?"

"The whole town's only been here for a short time," she giggled. "Come up from Sacramento 'cuz of the big silver strike but didn't like what I saw in Virginia City. The only thing expected of a woman was something I don't do. That's when I met Uncle Bob. He ain't a real uncle, you know that, don't you?"

Slim chuckled at the question. She had his full attention. Her face, more than lovely to start with was animated, fresh, and her eyes never left his. "He's not your uncle?" He gave her a little wink.

"No," she giggled. "He wanted to open a bakery and café but didn't quite have enough money. We ain't together, you know, like a man and woman. But we are partners in this little café. My folks were killed and left me enough to help buy this place. He says we brought some dignification to Washoe City." Both Slim and Celinda laughed at the word.

"Did the sheriff come in? Or Mockingbird?"

"Oh, yes. Sheriff Hansen came in often. So did Wilson. I liked him. He was funny and it always made the sheriff angry."

"Wilson?" Slim asked.

"Wilson Garrity, the deputy who was killed with the sheriff. Don't understand how the two of them could be mixed up with that nasty man, Crazy Ned Paulson. I thought it was Wilson told the sheriff that Paulson was in town. Now, all I hear is that the two of them were involved in the bank robbery. I was there. I never saw either one."

"You've just answered a whole passel of questions, Celinda. Thank you. I don't think either the sheriff or his deputy were involved. I think they were chasing Paulson and his gang and got ambushed. The whole thing is really confusing, though."

Calhoun was having a hard time taking his eyes away from the girl, wanted to know a lot more about her, and knew getting answers on the murder was more important. Still...

"I'd like to spend a lot more time talking with you, Celinda, but I really do need to get out and about, get answers to that killing." *She's so young and yet has her head square on those lovely shoulders. A man would have a hard time doing better, I think. Got some smarts, this girl does.*

"That would be nice, but I know you have work to do. Maybe we could talk some more, later," she said and his heart jumped a notch or two. The words were genuine as was the smile's invitation.

"I'll look forward to that," he stammered, fully taken aback by her response.

CHAPTER 13

"So, this is Big Maude's Pleasure Palace, eh?" Bull Morrison was standing in front of a gaudy building fitted out somewhat to look like a Mississippi River steamboat. "Whoever built this monstrosity ain't never been within a hunnert miles of the Big Muddy."

A broad porch narrowed to the double door entrance, which opened to a front parlor with hanging purple velvet curtains and purple velvet covered chairs and settees. The carpet was well worn by timber workers, miners, and mule-skinners. "Ugly," Morrison said right out. Three women were sprawled in the chairs, giving the marshal a good look at the wares being offered.

Off to the left of the entrance parlor was the bar area while just back from the parlor was a hallway leading to Big Maude's apartment and the kitchen. A stairway led to the second floor where the girls had their rooms. Bull couldn't keep the scowl off his face as the girls made their offerings.

"Not today, girls," he snarled. "Strictly business." He

forgot that earlier he had said they would just make this a friendly little visit. "Need to talk with Maude James." He pulled his marshal's badge and shoved it in the face of the nearest soiled dove. "Get her."

The young lady, covered in too much makeup and not covered where a society girl would be, jumped up and danced into a hallway toward the back of the building. Bull tried his best to smile and Duffy had to chuckle at the scene. *He has his ways.*

The other two ladies of the night followed the first one out of the room. "Scared 'em off, Duffy. Don't know why they'd be scared. This place ain't fit for man or beast. Stinks, too. Ain't never needed perfume, myself." Bull's thoughts were on the bar area, not perfume, and he found it strange that there weren't any customers in there drinking.

Duffy laughed right out, trying to get a picture of Bull Morrison dabbing himself with smelly perfume. "I doubt you have," he said through his laughter. He was catching his breath when Big Maude made her entrance.

"You the marshal?" she asked, looking squarely at Bull. She stood about five feet and four inches, but weighed a hefty one eighty if an ounce, he thought. Little pig eyes, three or four chins, and her hair was yellow, but surely not made so by God in heaven.

Crass. My god, the ladies in San Francisco would never work for someone like this. She should be ashamed. Bull took as shallow a breath of that horrible perfume as he could and nodded, showing her his badge. "I am. Heard that Ned Paulson spent the night before the bank robbery here. Need to ask a few questions about that."

"Lots of men spent the night here before the bank

robbery, Marshal. So what?" Her voice was not the soft voice of a lover, but that of a stevedore loading a three-master in a deep harbor somewhere. One who drank too much whiskey.

"The so-what part is this, Mrs. James." Bull leaned toward her, making her back up a step. "You spent some time with Paulson, had dinner with him is what I heard. Did he find out about the cabin in Parker Canyon from you? Did you give him permission to hide out there? How did the sheriff come to be involved?"

Bull Morrison almost shouted out the questions, just as fast as he could put the words together, and Big Maude stood her ground, glaring at the big man. "Ain't none of your business who I have dinner with, Marshal. I'll have dinner with anyone I choose." She ignored the other questions, and started to turn to walk off.

"Don't you walk away from me, woman. And the Parker Canyon cabin? According to county records, it is yours. Did you tell Paulson about it?"

She stopped and turned around, slowly, eyes about halfway closed, and smiled at Morrison. "Don't remember," she said, and turned, almost giving him the come on over her shoulder.

"By damn, woman, we're talking multiple murders and I want answers." Maude took one more step toward that door that led to the back of the building but turned toward Bull.

"Why'd the sheriff know to ride out there?" Bull asked

"Guess you'd have to ask him, Marshal. Good bye. I'm sure you can find your own way out."

Mike Duffy could remember Slim Calhoun's words and looked at Bull. *He's about to tear this place to shreds.*

Gotta get him out of here. "Let's not get riled, Bull. I think we need to have another talk with Mockingbird at the jail."

"Good idea. Can't understand any man would want to spend more than half a second with that fat pig." He stomped his way through the door and off the porch taking great deep breaths with each step. "Horrible place," he muttered more than once.

————

THERE WAS no one in the sheriff's office when they arrived. "Ain't been gone but a few minutes," Duffy said. "Fire's well stoked and the coffee's fresh." He grabbed two tin cups from a shelf and poured for the two of them. "Might be in the back. I'll go check."

He didn't have to as Mockingbird came through from the jail. "Thought I heard voices. Hello, Duffy, Bull. This town's alive with bad talk about the sheriff. Next they'll be accusing him of wife beatin'. You learn anything?" The old jailer slipped into the chair behind the sheriff's desk, reached into the lower right drawer and came up with a flask.

"Should be enough here for the three of us," he said. He didn't pour coffee in his cup and handed the flask to Bull who dumped his coffee back in the pot and filled his tin cup with the good stuff. Duffy got the remains and offered a growl and scowl back.

"Ain't learned nothing we could take to a judge," Bull Morrison said. "Tell me about Little Al Tyson. Other than what he calls his gang, who else in town seems somewhat close to him."

"He ain't close to nobody," Mockingbird said. "There

are those that want to be close to him, but he don't want to be close to nobody. Men like Jake James."

Bull smiled at the comment. Morrison had been trying to figure out how, maybe even why, he thought Big Maude, her husband Jake, and this Tyson outlaw might all be connected. "I've heard that Jake has a few heavies who work for him on small hit jobs. You think maybe Tyson and Jake work together?"

"That ain't what I said, Marshal." Mockingbird took a long drink and set the cup down. "What I said is, Jake is a small time heavy and Tyson runs a tight ship that Jake would like to be a part of."

Duffy caught Mockingbird's drift about the same time Bull did. "What's your call on either Little Al or Jake being a part of the Parker Canyon killings?"

"Ain't nothing I've heard to put either one of them anywhere near the canyon. Little Al could pull that off. I don't know if Jake could. On the other hand, the place is owned by Big Maude." He got up, grabbed a chunk of wood and moved Bull aside to shove it in the hot stove.

"Little Al's got a mean streak in him, Marshal. He takes pleasure in seeing someone in great pain. Sadistic is a mild word for the man. None of those dead men were tortured at all. Everyone died from a bullet wound or a knife. They were killed quickly, efficiently, not sadistically."

"You should have been the sheriff, not Dan Hansen," Bull Morrison said. He drank some whiskey and leaned back against the wall. *This Mockingbird fellow has a quick mind, but just gave us two different stories. First, he said Little Al could probably pull the killings off and then said the killings were not in Little Al's style. I wonder what Jake's style would be?*

"Something else, Marshal," Mockingbird continued. "This all came together mighty fast. Crazy Ned came to town the day before the robbery and spent the night at Big Maude's. Little Al wouldn't even have known he was in town, much less that he was about to rob the bank and head out for that cabin."

"You've got Jake James in your sights, eh? Yet, you say you didn't think Jake could put something like that together."

"That's right, Marshal, but he was good at following orders."

Bull sat quiet for a moment. *Good at following Big Maude's orders? She knew Paulson's plans, suggested he hide out at the Parker Canyon cabin, and Jake works for her.* "Thank you, Mockingbird. You've been a big help." *If what I'm thinking is what happened, that means the bank's money might be somewhere very close.*

Bull sat still contemplating everything that was said. If Jake James was the killer, was he following orders? Big Maude's orders? And if so, he would have brought all that bank money back to Big Maude. Bull Morrison had a hard time smiling what with that long knife wound scar across his face but at the moment, he was able to, just slightly. *I wonder where that big vault would be?* Mockingbird broke the reverie.

Mockingbird smiled. "Thank you. The county commission just appointed me acting sheriff until they can call an election. From what I saw at the scene and the bodies, this was an ambush, probably twice over."

"How's that? Twice over." Bull leaned in toward the jailer.

"I think Paulson was ambushed first and then the sheriff. What I don't understand is why those cowboys from the Franktown Valley ranch were there. And why they were killed. Big Maude owns a ranch in the Franktown area, but those cowboys were not known troublemakers. Jake used them for muscle once in a while, but nothing as serious as multiple murders. Them being there throws a big old knot in my thinking."

Duffy was slowly putting it together listening to the back and forth between Jessup and Bull. "We have a great need to have a long talk with Jake James. He seems to be at the center of a lot of what's been going on."

"And Big Maude," Bull said. "We won't get anywhere near Jake at Big Maude's," Bull said. "She'll have him well protected. We sure as hell didn't learn anything from that fat pig either." He sat back, drained his tin cup, and stood up. "Two questions, Mockingbird. Where does Big Maude keep her money and jewels? In a large vault somewhere? And, where might we find Jake?"

"He's been known to drink at The Timbers and also at the Lakeside Inn. I think I'd try the Lakeside Inn first. It's up near the cemetery." He chuckled, reaching for his empty cup. "The vault? She has her own separate apartment at the Pleasure Palace, so that would be my first guess. Ain't never been invited to that apartment, myself," he snickered, slapping the desk. "Sorry me, eh boys?"

Duffy and Bull were laughing as they left the sheriff's office. "Lakeside Inn it is," Bull said. "On the main North-South Road? That's that big set of rock buildings we passed heading toward Parker Canyon road?" Mockingbird nodded and Bull walked out of the office.

"Ain't too many buildings mean much to me," Bull

said. "That one was something I don't think I've seen before. Caught my attention right off."

Mike Duffy looked at the marshal and wondered what brought that on. "There's some mighty fine looking buildings in San Francisco, Bull. What's up with this one?"

"Don't know for sure, Duf. The rocks, I guess, and the timber. Together, rocks and timber, it's just special in my mind."

CHAPTER 14

Slim Calhoun stood in awe, watching men manhandle a large ponderosa pine log onto a skid, which then moved it along tracks by a steam engine toward a band saw blade. The engines were known as donkeys, which they had replaced several years ago. "That log is twenty feet long and must weigh tons," he said. He was standing with David Lee Waters, the manager of the Comstock Mill Company, leading the tour.

In the cold waters of Washoe Lake, just yards from this magnificent sawing machine, were at least fifteen or more logs the same size. Walters had just told Calhoun that the mines of the Comstock were voracious in their consumption of Sierra Nevada lumber.

Waters smiled and nodded. "They'll skin the bark then cut that log to order. Some of the mines want their timbers as large as ten by ten inches for the underground workings. Mr. Mackay is very specific on what he wants."

John Mackay and his partners, Fair, Flood, and O'Brien, owned and operated a conglomerate of mines on the Comstock. They were known as the Silver Barons, and often were complained of as controlling the stock markets in Virginia City and San Francisco as well.

"What do you mean by specific wants?"

"For instance," Waters said, "we've come up with a 'mine grade timber' for the mines. Knots are weak spots, so the timbers they want to hold up the mines, hundreds of feet underground, have few if any knots."

"I've never imagined an operation of this size, Mr. Waters," Slim said. "During our investigation of both the bank robbery and the multiple killings that followed, we've come across the name Alfred Tyson, sometimes called Little Al. We understand he worked for you a while back. What can you tell me about the man?"

"I hope I never have another one like him on the payroll. He's an uncouth animal in my opinion. Doesn't have a piece of kindness in his body. Sadistic, Marshal. A man of his size and strength would go a long way in this business. Look at those men down there. Hell, look at me. I've been doing this work for a long time."

Slim had to agree with that. David Lee Waters was about five-ten, weighed a solid two hundred pounds, and there wasn't an ounce of fat on the man. He wondered how Bull would stand up in a toe-to-toe fight with Mr. Waters. "You said sadistic. How so?"

"He seemed to get pleasure out of setting another worker up to get hurt. He seemed to take pleasure in seeing to it that machinery failed and in its failure hurt someone. He ridiculed men when they were injured, and berated others when they weren't quite as strong as he was. That man was strong, Marshal."

"What about friends? Did Tyson make friends while working here?"

"Not that I know of. There were those who wanted to be on his good side," Waters chuckled, "but not as friends. I don't think the man understands the word. He uses people but that's as close as they are allowed." David Lee Waters ushered the two of them into his office and motioned Slim toward a large over-stuffed chair.

"There was one man, Oberlin, I think. Yes, Frank Oberlin. Owns the Lakeside Inn, out near the cemetery. Oberlin left the mill here to build the little inn and saloon. It's right on the road connecting Carson City to Lake's Crossing. The road runs around and through Franktown, where the first mill was set up, and then back down into the valley. He and Tyson were often seen together just before some kind of accident happened."

"He and this Oberlin created accidents?"

"No," Waters said. "Tyson did. He and Oberlin had a falling out over those accidents."

―――――

SLIM CALHOUN'S head was filled with lumber mill workings, Little Al's sadism, and Frank Oberlin's rough ways as he rode off from the mill toward the north south highway. There were two north/south roadways, one on the west side of the lake, which ran up through Franktown where the first of the mills was built, and through the foothills of the sierra Nevada turning along the north shore of Washoe Lake before heading north toward Lake's Crossing.

The second road skirted close along the eastern edge of the lake with the Virginia Range running right down to the water's edge in places. The mills were along the north and north-east edges of the lake.

"Bull may have been lucky with his encounter with Little Al. The man is most dangerous." Slim had a long conversation with his horse making his way through Washoe City to the Lakeside Inn.

He had these thoughts that Little Al Tyson was heavily involved in the murders at Parker Canyon but couldn't get Tyson connected with either Big Maude or Crazy Ned. The connection of Jake James was obvious —he was Big Maude's husband—but Little Al didn't seem to have any connection.

"Then why do I have the sense that he is connected?" Calhoun said it right out, catching himself and snickered. *That was stupid. Not the question though.* The question of why he felt Little Al had any part of the bank robbery or murders that followed bothered the deputy marshal almost as much as to why all those murders took place. *There's a piece to this puzzle that someone has lost or destroyed.*

He rode up on a two story rock and timber building off the road a hundred yards or so. The lower story was all rock with deep inset windows. The upper story was roughhewn timber and clapboard siding. It was a charming building in a heavily timbered setting. *A man would be more likely to see something like this in the north-east, not Nevada Territory. Right at the eastern base of the Sierra Nevada.*

He saw two entrances, one marked Inn and Café, the other, Lounge. *Most saloon owners in Nevada Territory wouldn't use that word. More back east or San Francisco talk. Best start at the Lakeside Inn Lounge.* He spotted two horses tied off on the side of the building. *Bull and Duffy having a cocktail and waiting for me?* He laughed, tying off. *What brought them here?*

Around on the side, beside the waiting tie racks were two small barns, one filled with hay, the other with stalls. There were two corrals and directly behind the building, the privy. A balcony surrounded the upper story of the building with windows looking out on the lake and doorways onto the balcony. The balcony provided shade across the front of the first level.

The rooms must be on the two levels, he thought, looking at the ornate woodwork on the balcony. The rooms on the lower level had windows and doors leading out toward the corrals.

"He's got himself a comfortable inn for travelers," Calhoun muttered. "Might want to move from the hotel to out here, away from nosy town people." Again the thought of the northeast of the country came to mind. "This is an inn in the New England style of Maine or Vermont, he thought. No matter how he looked at it, the inn was out of place here but a welcome sight, indeed

Inside the Lounge, Slim found Bull and Duffy at the end of a short bar. The room was filled with tables, clean but empty, and there was a section set aside for poker and other gambling. "Fancy running into you two," he said, stepping up to the bar, nudging Bull just a bit.

"Want you to meet Frank Oberlin, Slim." Bull looked at Oberlin. "This is my partner, Deputy U.S. Marshal Slim Calhoun."

Oberlin barely nodded his head toward Slim. "Drinking?" was all he said.

"Mr. Oberlin is not in favor of our little visit, Slim. Prefers having Jake James or Little Al Tyson as customers." Bull had what he considered a smile on his face saying that. Slim and Oberlin saw a sneer. "Says he's never heard of Crazy Ned Paulson, neither. The road to Parker Canyon cuts the highway about fifty yards or so west of here but Mr. Oberlin says he's never heard of Parker Canyon."

Bull Morrison was having fun and Slim wondered just how long he and Duffy had been here. "Glad to meet you, Oberlin," Slim said. "Just left the Comstock Mill. You used to work there, right?"

He got no response from the owner of the Lakeside Inn. Slim couldn't put the man's total lack of warmth or greeting to what he saw in the design of the Lakeside Inn. "Did you design this place? It's well done. Seems like it should be in the mountains back east. New England somewhere."

"Vermont," Oberlin said, realized what he'd done, and took a couple of slow steps away.

"I didn't mean to get personal," Slim said. "It's just that I like what I've seen. I would like a whiskey, too."

Bull saw the change in Calhoun's approach, thought to himself that that was why he was his partner, and hoped that maybe they might learn something after all. Oberlin had been cold, not the least bit glad he had two paying customers on a windblown, snowing, winter's day. Bull looked at Duffy who had big eyes on Slim and knew the two of them would just stand at the bar and listen.

Oberlin turned, gave Slim a mean look, but slowly made his way back, put a glass up and a bottle. "Be a dollar," he said.

Slim eased a five-dollar gold piece onto the clean bar. "Never been to Vermont. Heard about the Green Mountain Boys." He looked around the Lakeside Inn Lounge, in particular the large rock fireplace blazing its warmth into the bar area. "Must have been quite a chore building these walls and that fireplace."

"Friends from the Comstock Mill helped," Oberlin said. "Brought the rocks from up on the ridge. Took us one whole summer to build this place."

Calhoun could almost feel the man opening up. This was his place and he was damn proud of it, wanted to talk about building it, and just maybe, might get some names, too. "Did you mill out these timbers, too? What a job that had to be." Slim looked at Bull. "Don't think there's a piece of construction that weighs less than five hundred pounds."

"Had some help," Oberlin said. "Old tired James needed a job, but that was before he locked up with fat Maude. He's a hard worker as long as you tell him what to do." He chuckled as if remembering something. "Jake James hasn't had an idea of his own in his life. He'll do an adequate job as long as you tell him how and when to do it." He stood looking at Slim, shaking his head, remembering that long summer of hard work.

"Him and Little Al, before he got all pushy. Won't even let Little Al in anymore. Man's got it in him to hurt anyone that wants to know him some."

Calhoun took a drink, thinking that Oberlin hadn't had a chance to have a decent conversation with anyone for a long time. It was like he had sprung a leak in the dam of conversation. *Ain't the time to slow the man down.*

"Old Jake and Little Al are friends? That surprises

me," Slim said. "What gave you the idea to build an inn like the ones back east?"

"Raised in one. Gramps built the Green Mountain Inn just like the one his gramps had. Whole family raised in Vermont inns. There's no more beautiful country in the world, you know. Should never have come west. Had it good and too dumb to know it," Oberlin said.

Calhoun saw sadness in the man's eyes and knew why he had such a bad attitude. Is he stuck out here in Nevada Territory? Not welcome back in Vermont? Owes too much money to be able to leave? Or something sinister, like taking part in a multiple murder along with Little Al and Jake James? "Seems to me you brought Vermont right along with you."

"Close as I'll get," Oberlin said. "You're right, though. Little Al and Jake ain't friends. They get along to a point. Little Al ain't got no friends. I tried being a friend, but Little Al thinks people are just toys to be played with." He reached behind him and pulled a bottle from the rack, up high, on its own pedestal and poured a drink for Slim and himself.

Bull took a deep breath. *That's the ultimate an inn keeper can do for a customer. That's a bottle of the best liquor the man has in the place and he's drinking it with Slim. Oh, you little buddy, you just keep that man talking.*

"Jake on the other hand needs friends. He's desperate for friends. Old fat Maude needed him, used him to get licensed, and he doesn't even know that. I could tell you stories of how Maude uses him, how Little Al almost killed the man half a dozen times." Frank Oberlin took a sip of his best bourbon and looked deep into Slim's eyes. What did he see? Slim on the other hand thought he saw a lonely man desperately seeking to return to his youth by way of this inn.

What was the man seeing? Or was he searching for something? The slightest smile crossed his heavy face, the glare in his eyes softened just a bit, and he took a second sip. "You boys are the marshals I've heard that are in town, eh? Come to pester old Frank Oberlin because he once worked with Little Al and helped get Jake James back on his feet after being released from San Quentin?

"Well, Slim Calhoun, I like your style. That big guy with the bad scar ain't much on talking nice, and the other'n is Texan and I don't much care for Texans. You looking for whoever left all them bodies up Galena Creek?"

"We are," Slim said. He couldn't keep the smile off his face and took a sip of the finest bourbon he'd ever tasted. "Whew. This, Frank Oberlin, is heaven in a bottle."

"It's magic, you know. Just like gold is magic." Oberlin poured just a bit more. A smile worked its way across a face unused to harboring a smile.

"Gold is magic?" Bull asked.

"Sure is." He picked up the five-dollar gold piece Slim had put down on the bar. "Take the meanest, nastiest wildcat of a woman and ease the gold into her hands and she magically becomes the softest, lovingest, little kitten you've ever met."

Bull Morrison chuckled and Slim laughed. Oberlin smiled and pocketed the gold coin. "I don't know one single thing about the bank robbery, about Crazy Ned Paulson, or about all the dead bodies they found up the creek. It would not surprise me that either Little Al or

Jake were involved. It would surprise me if they were working together."

"Why would that surprise you?"

"Because one, probably Little Al would kill the other. If they were working together, only one would be alive right now and that's the gospel."

Slim let all of that get settled in his brain before trying to say anything. He wondered if either Little Al or Jake James was involved. No, he thought, because of Big Maude, Jake has to be involved. Big Maude married Jake because she could manipulate him. Does she have the bank's money, and if so, how did she get it?

If she doesn't have all that gold and silver, who does? Where would they keep it? Are we missing something, like, maybe, someone we haven't even heard about? Slim Calhoun's mind was ripping out question by the score and nary an answer was found.

"You have a wonderful inn, Mr. Oberlin. I'd like to spend some time sitting in front of that fire some cold and stormy evening," Slim said. "Having a gentleman tell me stories about the Green Mountain Boys and the hills of Vermont."

"You'd be more than welcome, Marshal. You can even bring the big angry man with you." The smile was real and generous this time, and the three marshals slipped into their coats and headed for the roughhewn door. "Thank you," Oberlin said softly as the door closed.

"That man has stories bottled up deep, Bull. He doesn't have one thing to do with bank robberies, murdered robbers and lawmen, or Little Al's gang of thieves. Something far in his past is what's had him roped and tied."

"We need to talk with Jake James," Bull said. "We were told he might be here. If we should happen to walk into The Timbers, looking for Jake, you can buy the first round," Bull laughed. Slim Calhoun had to chuckle knowing that it was always that way.

"That five-dollar gold piece got us some answers all the cussing and pounding on the bar would never have. Interesting that Jake moved here after getting out of prison and worked for Oberlin before meeting up with Big Maude. I wonder what the connection is with Crazy Ned Paulson? Is it with Big Maude or with Jake James?"

"That one I can answer," Mike Duffy said. "The connection is Singin' Sammy, or, if you prefer, Crazy Ned. It was Singin' Sammy what sent Jake to prison. They robbed a bank south of San Francisco and the coppers nailed Sam who immediately gave up on Jake. Jake did three years' hard time."

"Ahh," said Bull. "Jake has to be our man. Pay back is hell and the devil came calling in Parker Canyon."

"That fits fine, Bull." Slim had a smile on his face despite the driving snow and ice. "Now, my fine friend, let's prove it. Find the terrible Jake James and ease the truth from him."

They couldn't see twenty feet in front of them but Mike Duffy knew the way to The Timbers and led them in. "Wonder how these storms build up so fast. I was at the mill just a few hours ago and watched the clouds boil over those high mountains," Slim said. "This one's gonna be with us for a while, I'm thinking."

CHAPTER 15

"Oberlin is a most interesting man," Bull Morrison said. "Glad you stopped by, Slim. Wouldn't have gotten a word out of the man if you hadn't." They were in their saddles walking their horses slowly back to the heart of Washoe City.

You're right, Bull. Slim chuckled at the thought. *Most of the time your way works well. The name Bull is the personality, but sometimes, it's best to go in easy and slow.* "That man Oberlin was waiting for someone like me, Bull. I liked that place and he could feel that. He and I will have more than this one discussion."

"I can't remember ever seeing the kind of work that was done there. I'm not just impressed," Bull said, "I'm in awe. To be able to fit the rocks, to carve the timber, to mold the wrought iron..." He just let his thoughts drift off into the heavy snow pounding the men. Slim didn't think he had ever seen Bull's face as serene as it was at that moment.

I've been his partner for a long time, now, I've known that the man has a heart, has feelings, is even empathetic from time to time, but this reaction is something new. Was Slim Calhoun seeing a mellowing out of Bull Morrison? Bull would laugh in your face if you suggested it.

"I think we were led down the wrong path though," Duffy said. "We won't be finding Jake James having cocktails at the Lakeside Inn. Not with the reaction we saw from Frank Oberlin."

"Whoever told you that was probably thinking of the times when Jake worked there. Before Big Maude," Slim said. "What has me confused in all this is Little Al. Known for being sadistic yet none of those men who were murdered at the Parker Canyon cabin were tortured. And, then we have Jake James."

"He's high on my list," Bull said. "Very high being tied so tight with Big Maude and her being close to Crazy Ned Paulson."

"I agree," Slim said. "Except for what Frank Oberlin just told us. He said Jake never had a creative or even a thought of his own, only did what he was told. That combination of killings at the cabin were planned by someone with a very good mind."

"Like Big Maude's," Mike Duffy said.

"Like Big Maude's," echoed Slim. "She and Paulson have supper before the robbery, he runs for the Parker Canyon cabin she owns, and she sends Jake to kill the gang and recover the money. The sheriff interferes and is eliminated."

"Oberlin said something about Jake being released from San Quinton. Let's not forget Crazy Ned's real name. Sam Sampson. Singing Sammy Sampson. Singing Sammy sent Jake James up the river. Revenge can be sweet, I've heard." Duffy chuckled at his words.

"A chance to get even and grab the bank loot?" Bull

said. "He wouldn't have needed much prodding from Big Maude."

"So, then," Slim said. "Where's the money?" He got no answer as the three rode down the main street of Washoe City.

"My first thought is a bottle of rot gut at The Timbers," Bull said, "but my stomach is crying out for food. Bear steaks this big or half a roasted pig, or both would fit me fine right now."

"Uncle Bob's Café it is, then," Duffy said, nudging his horse into a trot. Bull Morrison sunk his spurs, gave a wild yell, and led the three through town to Uncle Bob's, at a full gallop, chasing the few people out walking in the snow off the roadway, all three sliding their horses to a stop at the tie rack.

"Damn me but I can smell roasted pig clear out here," Bull said.

Celinda O'Mally watched the three jump from their horses, laughing and jostling each other like little boys showing off for whoever might be watching. She gave Slim Calhoun a generous smile when they burst through the doors. "My goodness," she said.

"It's a good day, Miss O'Mally," Slim said, returning her smile.

Her eyes were alive and shining, her knees were weak, and she had to turn away or she'd throw her arms around the big marshal and make a fool of herself right here in her own café. "Mockingbird Jessup is having his mid-day meal at a window table. Would you like to join him?"

"Indeed we would," Bull said and walked straight to the table. "Glad you're here, Jessup. Got some ideas to bounce off you."

"I have some, too, Marshal."

Bull's eyes devoured the several slices of elk roast on Mockingbird's plate, and he grabbed extra chairs for the bunch. "Elk roast, eh? I was going to have me a big old bear for dinner but half an elk would be just fine."

Celinda had no trouble getting everyone's order. "You gentlemen would be satisfied if I just started bringing platters of food, no matter what kind, just as long as the platters were heaping, right?"

"That's one smart lady, Slim," Duffy said. "Might want to get to know her better."

"I'm planning on it," Slim said as quietly as he could. She heard him, though, took a quick breath, turned a nice color of red, and danced back into the kitchen. Bull didn't see any of that, was rather, staring at Mockingbird's roast elk.

———

An hour later, three marshals and an appointed sheriff found their way through a heavy snow storm to The Timbers. "Does the sun ever shine in Washoe Valley?" Bull asked.

"Only when the wind blows," Jessup laughed. "And that's most of the time in the spring, summer, and fall. We're in the winter, Bull. That's when it rains and snows." He was laughing remembering that the wind blew at gale force or better most of the time.

"The first of the men working in what's now Virginia City called our winds the Washoe Zephyr as a joke. These aren't zephyrs my friend, these are hurricane winds that'll strip you naked if you try to stand against them." Mockingbird laughed.

"Snow's bad enough," Duffy said, pushing his way into The Timbers. The place was busy, probably because of the storm that blew in. Mill workers, teamsters, a few cowboys, and of course the local town drunks all gathered for late afternoon cocktails.

Bull was the pathfinder and led them through the throng to an open spot at the bar. He shoved a couple of men aside and the four filled the space. "Looks like bad weather ain't bad for business," Duffy said. "Haven't seen Jake."

"I thought I saw him when we walked in," Slim said, "but I don't see him now. Think he slipped out seeing us come in?"

"I would have," Bull said. Bull caught the barman's eye, ordered a bottle, glasses, and beers around for the four. He nodded to the barman that Slim would be paying.

"Seen Jake James around this afternoon?" Bull asked.

"Glad to say, no, I haven't," the man replied. "Usually brings trouble when Big Maude lets him off the leash. Fact is, he gets to drinking at Maude's place and she kicks him out to cause trouble here. You the sheriff now, Mockingbird?"

Jessup nodded and started to say something. "You need to put that woman out of business," the barman continued. "That place is a pigsty and her so-called husband is a trouble maker. Needs closing," the barman said, walking down the bar to help others.

"He's upset because Big Maude's girls get more action than the girls here, do," Jessup laughed. "Been cry-babying about Big Maude from the day she opened."

"He's got a point," Bull said. "That place ain't healthy for man or beast."

"She's raking in big money, Bull," Jessup said. "County could write some laws based on health, I suppose, but she ain't breaking no laws right now."

"What's all the excitement out there?" Mike Duffy stepped back from the bar and tried to get a clear view out the front doors. Men were hollering, some running out the doors while others started moving toward them.

"Best go check it out," Duffy said. Slim, Bull, and Mockingbird followed him, joining the crowd. "There you are, Mockingbird," someone yelled from the street when they walked out. "Been a murder, Sheriff, down at the Comstock Mill. Better hurry."

"Want to bet it's Jake's body we'll find?" Bull snickered stepping into his saddle. The four men worked their horses through the crowd and made good time on the quick run to the lake's edge. Mill workers were standing in the raging snow storm and parted as they rode to the manager's office.

David Lee Waters met them, wrapped in a bearskin great coat and fur hat. "Ain't never had anything this horrible happen at the mill, Marshal. "Come, it's horrible, just horrible." Waters was a big man, had been working in timber most of his life, but whatever had happened had brought the man almost to weeping, wringing his hands, tears evident on his rugged face.

They walked through the crowd of workers and looky-loos, actually shoving some aside, and made their way into the main building where the great logs were sliced to order. Snow was being driven by the tempest and looking out across the waters, white caps were sending froth into the maelstrom creating even more chaos.

"Over here," Waters said, walking up to where the logs were dragged from the lake and onto the cutting trolley. Bull eased the manager away and he and Calhoun took the few steps down to the water's edge. There, tied on her back to a log, legs spread wide, arms wrenched around toward the back of the slim log, was Big Maude James, a neat hole in the middle of her forehead.

"She's been in the water for some time," Jessup said.

"Water washed away the blood," Slim said. "She's been dead for more than a day."

"She had to have been killed not long after our visit, then," Bull said. His thoughts went immediately to Jake. "This has to be Jake's work."

"I'm not sure, Bull," Slim Calhoun said. "Remember Little Al has mill work experience. He would know that it might be a day or two before the body was found."

"All of this is tied to the bank robbery and ain't none of us has any idea where that money might be," Mike Duffy said. "We might think it's in Big Maude's vault but ain't none of us knows that. And, like Frank Oberlin said, if Little Al's involved, anybody who might think he's a partner is gonna die." He took a long pause, looking at the others and at what was left of Big Maude. "We ain't seen Jake, on the one hand, and what we're seeing now, Maude's killer is a sadistic bastard at best."

Calhoun looked at Bull and they both had the same idea. "Mockingbird, you and Mike Duffy handle this end of our job. Bull, we got to get up to Big Maude's Pleasure Palace and I mean right now. If that money really was in that vault of hers, I'll bet it's gone now."

"We'll all meet at Uncle Bob's later this evening. Let's go, Slim."

"We want a full investigation of this, Duffy," Slim said. "We want to know everything you can find out about how she died, was she tortured first, is there even a shred of evidence pointing right at someone. This is gonna rock this community."

Bull shuddered at that comment. The sheriff was dead following a major bank heist. Was he involved? The robbers were dead and the money was missing. Big Maude knew where the robbers would be hiding after the robbery. Was she involved? Where was the money? And now, Big Maude's body had shown up.

"We don't got a lot of time to put this all together, Bull. Because of the sheriff's involvement and Big Maude's untimely death, the politicians are gonna get involved."

Bull could see that the local government officials would start breathing down their necks if they couldn't come up with some answers and soon. "I'm not willing to put my thoughts to Jake or to Little Al right now. But we had best start coming up with answers damn quick. I think you nailed it pretty good, Slim. Let's ride."

CHAPTER 16

BULL HAD A LOOK THAT SAID SOMETHING LIKE, 'YOU handle this. I'm going to kill one of these broads in a minute.' Slim Calhoun had to chuckle watching the big man try to bully the working girls at Big Maude's Pleasure Palace. Some of the girls were having a good time getting the big man riled, while others simply didn't give a damn.

The entry parlor was small and Slim had everyone settled in in the bar area. On what might be considered a normal day, Jake would be behind the bar and Big Maude would be stationed at the end, keeping close watch over things.

When the marshals arrived, they immediately closed the place, chased a couple of paying customers off, and brought all the girls into the parlor first in order to tell them about the murder of Maude. They hadn't reached that point, and the girls were angry at these men shutting off their income, and didn't believe they had that authority.

"Where's Jake?" Slim asked, looking around the

gaudy and not very clean room. The greeting room of this whorehouse was a shambles in the middle of the afternoon. Later at night, after a bit too much to drink, it might seem hospitable. "I told you I wanted everyone here. Where's Jake?" They had searched the bar area, not finding anyone in there, not even a barman.

"He hasn't been around all day, Marshal. Left sometime late yesterday afternoon," one of the working girls said. She said her name was Naomi and she couldn't have been twenty, slightly overweight, with big eyes, a mean little mouth, and dull, limp hair. She had eyes for Bull Morrison and he wasn't having any of it. She thought she was teasing the big man. He thought he just might shoot her.

"I don't suppose he mentioned where he might be going?" Bull asked. When Bull asked a question, it was never a gentle little affair. It was more like, answer me now or die. His eyes blazed, his entire being was a menace to whomever he was asking. "Well?"

Naomi scuttled back a step or two, burst into tears, and Bull just threw his hands up. "You take over, Slim, before I kill someone." He walked into the bar and sat down at one of the tables, drumming his fingers on the wood.

Slim wanted to chuckle at Bull's reaction but also was aware that the girls hadn't been told about Big Maude's demise yet. "Let's all move into the bar, shall we?" It took a few minutes to get re-organized and Slim dropped the bomb.

"There's been a tragedy, ladies, that we all need to discuss. Please, sit down and listen good, then we'll be asking some questions." He looked at Bull, his eyes telling the big man to calm down, not put the fear of death into the girls, and let's work through this.

"Big Maude's body was found just hours ago near the Comstock Mill." This wasn't the time to try to make this easy on anyone. Too many people had died, too much money was unaccounted for. And there hadn't been any answers to so many questions.

Gasps, whimpers, and crying erupted from the five women spread across the barroom of the Pleasure Palace. Some were sitting at drinking tables, some standing near gambling tables, and some were at the bar. Slim noticed that a few of the women didn't seem to have any reaction at all.

"I'll be brief," Slim continued. "There is no doubt that Maude was murdered, probably sometime after we left here yesterday." He didn't go into the grotesque details of the murder but looked closely at each of them. Big Maude was a big woman, probably almost as strong as she was big, and he was trying to picture each of these working girls as being able to maul the woman. None seemed to fit the bill. "Did Maude leave here after we left?"

The girls looked about at each other, before Bull snapped, again, "Well?" He started to get up and Slim motioned him down.

"Please, ladies. Did Maude leave here after we did?"

Naomi looked at Bull Morrison and cringed before answering. "She rarely leaves here and I don't think she did yesterday, either." She looked around and the others nodded in agreement.

"Don't matter none whether she left or not," the girl called Sweet Maria said. "What matters right now is what happens to us? That fat old woman owes me a lot of money. Ain't got my share for a week now. Who's gonna run this place?" Sweet Maria was in her early twenties, slim and attractive. She had big hands, Slim noticed right away.

She's spent a lot of time earlier in her life working hard. Probably on a family farm somewhere. He mulled that over for a quick moment. *How did Sweet Maria end up here? Each of these women must have stories to tell and it looks like their employment may have just ended.*

"My guess is Jake would take over unless Maude made other arrangements," Slim said to Maria. "I'm sure questions of money will get answered, but right now I'm far more interested in finding the person responsible for Maude's death." He stood up and walked around the large saloon, looking at each of the working girls as he passed.

"Well, then, did she have any visitors, let's say, other than customers?" Slim asked. Again, it was Naomi who answered that no, there were no visitors. It was Bull who brought up the main question.

"Was Jake here?" All the girls either nodded or said yes, and Bull tried his best to smile. "Take us to where Maude and Jake lived. I believe someone said they had a separate apartment or group of rooms here."

"I'll take you," Naomi said. She stood up to lead them out, making sure that there was someone between her and that big angry marshal with the bad scar. They walked down a long hallway with doors on either side where some of the girls had their rooms. At the back, there was a rather ornate, hand-carved door that was locked. Naomi tried it twice to prove the point.

"Who would have the key?" Slim asked.

"Both Big Maude and Jake have keys. None of us

do," Naomi said. "They keep the door locked even when they're inside. They don't want us around."

"That's right," Sweet Maria said. "We're only good for making money. Mattress backs we are. Money making mattress backs. We ain't to be seen in their special little home-sweet-home." Her bark of a laugh drew giggles from some of the others. Slim wondered just what the atmosphere must have been around the place.

"Get out of the way then," Bull said. He stepped back a few paces and drove his massive body into the hardwood door and actually bounced back two steps. "Well, just damn me," he said. If he heard Slim chuckle, he ignored it. "You're gonna lose, door."

It took three more full body attacks before the door finally splintered away from ornate wrought iron hinges. Bull kicked pieces of the door and its jamb away and looked over to Slim and offered just the slightest smile. Maybe he did hear the chuckles. "Where does Maude keep her safe?" Slim saw him gently rubbing his right shoulder.

Naomi took in a deep breath at the question and pointed toward a set of double doors which would normally be closed and locked, but were standing open. The doors opened into a closet which was filled by a large vault, also standing open.

Slim got down on his knees in front of the vault, giving the insides a complete once over. "Not even one shred of paper in here." He looked at the heavy open door, saw that it had a combination lock. "Who besides Big Maude has the combination?"

"No one," Naomi said. She looked around at the others and they all nodded their agreement.

"Not even Jake?"

There were assorted giggles from some of the girls, including Naomi. "Especially Jake," she almost whispered.

"What does that mean?" Bull Morrison looked at the front of the vault, at the sides, and along the seams. "This was opened by way of the combination. Why wouldn't Jake have it? He is her husband, right?"

Naomi cleared her throat, looked quickly at the other ladies, and then to Bull standing next to Slim. "Yes, Jake is married to Maude, but he is actually just a hired hand. She needs a husband to have this place licensed by the county. He's her husband in name only. He does what he's told to do and is punished often when he screws up." There were giggles from a couple of the girls and outright laughter from others.

"He tries to lord it over us," Sweet Maria giggled. "Thinks he's special but we just laugh at him. He ain't man enough to put his paws on us. That fat old woman thinks he's a fine lover. He's her love slave," she laughed and the others joined. "Love slave," they whispered over and over.

"And he doesn't have the combination," Slim said. "Would Maude just leave the vault open like this?"

"Never," Naomi said. "He must have forced her to open it."

"He?" Bull said. "You're assuming it was Jake who stole all the money and killed Big Maude? Don't spread that around. We'll be the ones to say who is behind all this." His flash of anger quieted the girls as he looked around at them, his eyes blazing again. "No one is blaming anyone, yet. You said Maude didn't have any visitors and that she rarely left this place. If that's the case, we know she did. She had visitors who forced her to unlock the vault. She had visitors who murdered her and made her leave, and someone left with her along with the contents of that vault. Did any of you see anything out of line at all yesterday?"

It was so quiet Slim had to cough to make sure his ears were still working. The girls were all looking back and forth at each other, shaking their heads, not saying a word. "I can't get this picture in focus," Slim said. "You're telling me that Big Maude, with everything that was in that safe, walked out of this building sometime yesterday and nobody saw her?"

"We have a liar standing close, Slim. Ain't possible." Bull was still thinking that the money from the bank had been in that safe. *Hundreds of pounds of gold and silver along with all the money this joint makes, is carried out of here by an obese woman and nobody saw it?* "One or more of you is lying and I'll get to the truth," Bull snarled.

He turned suddenly and the girls actually jumped back. "That's right," Bull said. "It is time to be frightened, girls. Not of me, I've never purposely hurt a woman, but of the consequences of lying to me. Prison ain't fun, ladies, and you lie to a federal marshal and if you don't die you go to prison." He went out of his way to look at each of the women. "Get the picture?"

Slim, too, was sure the money from the bank had to be in that safe, that that was why Maude was dead, that was why somebody was lying. "We need to know where Jake is, ladies. One or more of you know, one or more of you saw something yesterday. My partner is easily riled when he doesn't get answers to his questions. We don't want to have that happen."

The threat was in front of them, looming large, and each of the women could almost feel those huge hands of Bull Morrison doing considerable damage. "Who saw something," Slim asked. "Who knows something? If you're protecting someone, we'll find out and you'll spend years in prison if you live."

The girls spent some time looking around the room, at each other, at Bull, at Slim, before one of them finally spoke up. "I saw her and someone else carrying feed sacks yesterday but I didn't know they were leaving the building," a girl named Suzie said. "I just thought it was laundry sacks. I wasn't lying," she whimpered. She had a terrified look on her face and was pleading with Slim to call Bull off.

"Thank you, Suzie," Bull said. "Did you recognize who was with Maude?"

"No," Suzie said. "I really didn't think anything of it so wasn't paying much attention. It could have been Jake, it could have been anyone. I really don't know."

"What did he look like? How big? How tall? What color hair? What was he wearing? Come on, girl, tell us something." Bull's frustration level had risen once again.

"He might have been as big as you," Suzie said, cringing back, trying not to cry. She was blubbering, wiping tears away, and slowly sank into one of the velveteen covered chairs. "I don't know..." Her voice trailed off to a whimper.

"As Deputy U.S. Marshal for this territory, I'm closing this place until Big Maude's murderer is caught. Nobody leaves town." Bull again looked each girl in the eye. "Do you understand? Nobody leaves town." They all nodded. Some were crying softly, others just sitting looking at the walls with dull eyes. Sweet Maria was scowling, her angry eyes boring into Bull Morrison's.

"We can't just live here and not make any money." Sweet Maria wanted to get right in Bull's face but backed off a bit when he turned to her. She shook off his angry scowl and continued. "What about food and stuff?" She just wouldn't back all the way down. Even Bull eased off.

"She's right, Slim," Bull said. He looked her right in the eye. "All right, then, Sweet Maria, you are now in charge. I just rescinded my order closing the joint. Clean it up, keep it clean, no rough stuff with customers who drink too much, and you can re-open. Don't let me hear bad talk coming about this place."

He turned and strode out of the apartment, down the hall, and toward the front door to the loud cheers from the working girls and a few decidedly mirthful chuckles from Slim Calhoun. Sweet Maria had a grand smile, thinking that the big angry man might not be so mean after all, that it was just his way.

CHAPTER 17

"WHAT DID YOU FELLERS LEARN FROM YOUR investigation at the mill?" Bull, Slim, Mike, and Acting Sheriff Mockingbird were in the sheriff's office later that evening. "Hope you learned something," Bull said. "We sure as hell learned nothing."

"That's not true, Bull, and you know it," Slim said. "You need to relax. This isn't going to fall together that easy, so ease off. We need your brain in good working order, not flying off into the clouds somewhere."

Bull Morrison tightened up visibly, his mouth opened and he was about to tear into his deputy when he suddenly seemed to change his mind. "I'm tied up like a pig going into the boiling pot, Slim. Got the rumbles working through my brain. That scene at the Parker Canyon cabin's got me by the throat. The sheriff and his deputy is one group, Crazy Ned and his gang another, and what's got me in a pickle are those two ranch hands. What the hell were they doing there? Who instigated all that?"

He looked around the room and knew he had three

fine investigators sitting around the stove. *I've been working with Calhoun for several years, known Duffy a long time, and this Mockingbird Jessup will wear a badge for some years coming. How many times have I walked up to a crime scene and been physically repulsed? Only once and that was just day's ago.*

"You're right, Slim. I gotta calm down and think. Just can't get that scenario out of my mind."

He sat in a chair near the fire. "And now we have Big Maude, hogtied to a log, a bullet between her eyes and not a single answer yet." He looked straight at Slim Calhoun. "Tell me what we found today," He chuckled, feigned a punch to Slim's shoulder, and tried his best to smile.

Slim took a cup of coffee offered by Mockingbird Jessup and continued. "We found Maude's safe opened and empty and learned that only she had the combination." He nodded and smiled. "We learned that she was seen leaving the place with an unidentified man and they were carrying feed sacks that seemed to be filled with something heavy."

"Damn," Mike Duffy said. "All we came away with was that Maude was severely beaten before she was murdered. It appeared to both Mockingbird and me that she was tied to that log before she was shot. The woman was fully terrorized, Slim. One of her arms was broken, and that happened before she was tied to the log."

"Probably why she gave up the combination to her safe," Bull said. "The man who left with Maude was described as being about my size or so. Both Jake and Little Al might fit that description." He seemed to get just a bit contemplative and Slim liked seeing that. For

Slim, it meant the man was thinking, not just getting angry.

"What's that brain of yours working on?" Slim asked.

"Little Al has been described as being willing to torture someone. The word sadistic has been used over and over. We haven't heard that about Jake. Little Al is larger than I and the girls pointed out that they didn't recognize the man leaving with Maude and the money. They would have recognized Jake immediately, I would think."

"I think it's time to go on a hunt, gentlemen," Slim said. "I'm also thinking there was someone else hauling sacks out the door. A third person, Bull, someone who's name hasn't come up." He looked at Bull who was nodding slowly, putting what Slim said together with what he was already thinking.

"You're thinking that one of the girls might be involved, aren't you? That's damn good, Slim. One large man and Maude would have had difficulty moving all those sacks of gold. Hell, Paulson had three with him," he laughed. "Keep going, Slim. I like this."

"What I'm seeing is one large man, and probably Jake, manhandles Big Maude into giving him the combination while one of the girls keeps an eye out for anyone coming. They grab the sacks, force Big Maude to help carry them out."

"And Sweet Maria sees them," Bull said.

"Or it was Sweet Maria. I'm thinking Jake and another man along with Sweet Maria pulled this off. I don't think Little Al was involved. He's far bigger than you, Bull."

"He had to be involved," Duffy said. "It had to be

Little Al who forced the combination from Big Maude. Everything else you said I agree with, though. "I think Jake and Little Al have partnered up and Sweet Maria is in with them."

It was quiet in the sheriff's office as each of them knew what a tremendous effort it would take to put Little Al Tyson into irons. All had seen Bull Morrison in action, able to take on two, even three men at a time and come out victorious. And, they all knew that Little Al was bigger, maybe even stronger than Bull Morrison.

"I agree," Bull said. "I'm with you, Slim, but I'm not willing to take Jake off the hook. There are lots of arrows pointing at Little Al, but I think just as many leveled at Jake. Maybe Jake hasn't been known for being in favor of torture, but that doesn't mean he hasn't used it. We just don't know. We don't know what took place in that room where the vault is." He tried to smile, tried his best and only his eyes softened, not his angry mouth. "Sweet Maria. She tried to throw us off the track, Slim. Damn near made it, too."

Slim smiled and gave his boss a long look. "You're thinking about the cabin at Parker Canyon again, aren't you?"

"I am," Bull said. "That series of attacks were well thought out and accomplished, not the work of someone involved in sadistic behavior. The follow up on Maude, that is, tying her to a log so grotesquely is very sadistic. We think the money from the bank robbery was taken from Crazy Ned at Parker Canyon, possibly by Jake at Maude's demand. You with me so far?"

All nodded that they thought he was right. "Now we believe that money was taken from Maude's vault by

Little Al? How did Little Al know about that money? Am I seeing Jake working with Little Al?"

Don't forget Sweet Maria, Bull, Mike Duffy thought. *She might be the connection with Little Al.*

"Remember what Frank Oberlin at the Lakeside Inn told us. If Jake tied up with Little Al, Jake would die." Slim said. *I need to keep Bull thinking. His mind is fast and he might just be on something. The two of them working together would be fearsome.*

"He did say that," Bull said. "I think what took place at that cabin in Parker Canyon was plotted out by someone else and committed by Jake. We've been told several times Jake doesn't have an idea of his own in his head, but when told what to do is very good at following through. I'm of the opinion that Jake was the killer at the cabin and the plan was Maude's. She wanted that bank money."

"She did," Mockingbird said. "Had supper with Crazy Ned, even suggested he head to her cabin at Parker Canyon."

"And Jake didn't get any of that money after he killed all those men," Slim said. "Reason enough to rough up the lady and get the combination to the safe. He was carrying a load of anger toward the woman, Bull. Maude treated him like a slave is what the girls said. She ridiculed him right to his face, is what they told us. He had reason to get even. If that's the case, Bull, I'll repeat your question. How does Little Al fit in?"

"Damned if I know," he laughed right out. "Only by the way she was killed. That was sadistic. Maybe Jake needed Little Al as the threat to get the combination and Little Al followed through after getting the money. Oberlin said he enjoyed hurting people."

"And we don't know where either one is." Mike Duffy said.

Slim got up and walked all the way around the room, poured some coffee, and sat back down. "If we remember that Frank Oberlin told us that if Jake partnered up with Little Al Tyson, that Tyson would surely kill Jake as soon as possible after getting the money."

"You're right, Slim," Bull said. "That means that Jake is probably dead. If they partnered up. Here's what we need to do. Find Jake, alive or dead, and find Little Al. One of them will have the bank money and whatever money was in Maude's vault."

Slim looked around the room. "Mike, how about you and the sheriff find Jake and me and Bull will find Little Al?"

Bull got one of his almost smiles listening to Slim. He liked it that Slim didn't say try to find, he said, find Jake. Find Little Al. *There's no trying in the marshal Service,* Bull thought. *There's only doing.*

Let's start at The Timbers, Mike," the sheriff said. "I'm dry as one of your wind-blown Texas tumbleweeds."

––––––––

"Snow's gonna be more than a foot deep come morning, Slim. I'm hungry and you haven't seen that cute little Celinda O'Mally for hours."

"She's a bundle, Bull. Half owner of that place and never slows down. I wonder what she might know of Jake's movements or if she's seen him lately. Remember that Crazy Ned had breakfast in there the morning of the robbery. Maybe Jake was a customer, too."

Wind was blowing hard, driving the snow at close to fifty miles an hour down the long street to Uncle Bob's. Washoe Valley should have been named Windy Valley. "Simply couldn't live here, Slim. Middle of the day and you can't see the lake. Can't see them ten-thousand foot ridges of the Sierra Nevada and they should be right there," he said, pointing west.

The Carson Range of the Sierra spiked straight up from Washoe Valley, and Bull was right, on a clear day you could see that range plain as day. "There are hundreds of square miles of timber and rock right over there, where a man could hide out and never be caught. Eat deer, catch fish, live like a prince."

"We need to eat something fast, Bull, and ride like the wind for that cabin in Parker Canyon."

"To hell with eating, partner," Bull exploded, turning for the stables and almost running through the blizzard. "Time's a-wasting, Slim. You nailed it."

Slim reached out after a few long steps and stopped the big man. "No, Bull, we ain't going on a death ride. This is a blizzard. Can't see twenty yards in any direction. If either Jake or Little Al are at that cabin, they can't go anywhere either. They be as stuck as we are. Let's get some good hot food in us and do some serious planning."

Bull and Slim were standing in the middle of the main street, snow and ice blasting through the thin air, cold driving deep into their heavy buffalo robe coats, staring at each other. Bull broke first. He stood, shoulders slumped, frozen snot dripping from his nose, eyebrows ice sculpted into a scowl, and a little boy grin on his ugly face.

"I hate it when you're right, Slim, but you are. It

would be a death ride. We need a mule for packing, supplies for several days, and to wait for the end of the storm. Let's get something to eat."

They were the only ones out walking and forced their way through the storm driven snow, slipping on ice under the snow, fighting through drifts being built higher by the minute, and made their way into Uncle Bob's, struggling to get the door fully closed.

"Damn!" Bull almost shouted out, having to use his already sore shoulder to get the heavy door closed. He looked around, hoping nobody heard him, and worked to get his ice laden coat off. "Must burn ten cords of wood a month to keep this place warm," he joshed, getting settled at a table that looked out on the stormy scene outside.

Uncle Bob Lively peeked his head around the corner from the kitchen. "Thought I heard a moose come in. Evening, Marshal," he said with about a half smile. He looked from Bull Morrison to the front door, made sure it wasn't splintered, and pointed at the hand scrawled menu written on a blackboard. "Stew" is all it said.

"Celinda will be with you in a minute, gentlemen. I'll get you started with some coffee."

"Wouldn't have a bottle to go along with that coffee, would you?" Bull asked.

"We're not licensed for that," Uncle Bob said.

"We sure won't tell anyone," Bull said. "I promise." He reached up and put his hand over his Marshal's shield, chuckling softly.

Uncle Bob brought the coffee pot and a bottle to the table, laughing with the marshals. "Save some for me, Marshal," he said and headed back to the kitchen.

"Storms like these usually blow themselves out in a

day or two," Slim said. "Whoever's at the cabin, if anyone, can't leave any more than we can, so let's put them aside for the moment. Where else might Little Al or Jake for that matter, hide in a blizzard like this one?"

"Only two places I can think of," Bull said. "Little Al's joint at the south end of the lake or the Lakeside Inn. Little Al's place would be a damn hard ride. Oberlin's place not so much."

"Any place up Franktown Road where someone could set up camp?" Slim asked and caught Celinda coming out of the kitchen, saw the big smile and dancing eyes, and hoped this storm would last another few weeks.

"Evening, boys," she said. She laid her hand on Slim's shoulder and leaned, almost suggestively into him. "I was afraid the storm would keep you away. Got a couple of bear steaks left, Bull, and a big pot of beef stew. What's your pleasure?"

Slim looked into those fascinating eyes, did not say what was really on his mind, and said, simply, "The whole pot of stew, please."

She laughed, "And you get what's left of the bear, Mr. Bull, sir." She slipped away from Slim as he attempted to get his arm around her hips, and headed for the kitchen.

"Back to Franktown," Slim said, his eyes still on the kitchen door. "Judge Hyde's old lumber mill, just a relic, would make for decent hiding, and the Dall stamp mill, but it's still working. There are some fine ranches in those hills, though. It would be as hard to get to right now as Parker Canyon."

"We'll start at the Lakeside Inn," Bull said.

Celinda brought their plates and Slim asked her

about Jake. "Does he come in here? No one's seen him since the discovery of Big Maude's murder."

"Don't know much about the man. Don't want to, neither, Slim. He's a slimy snake in my opinion. Sucks hind tit off Big Maude who probably gets her fun out of beating on him. He does come in once in a while but Uncle Bob serves him, not me. You think he killed her?"

Slim gave her a big smile. "We want to talk to him about several things, Celinda."

"He was awfully close to Frank Oberlin before Maude took him under her skirts." She bent down and brushed his cheek with her lips and danced off before he could wrap his arms around her. Bull was laughing right out, trying to stuff half a bear in his mouth.

————

DUFFY AND MOCKINGBIRD bellied up to the bar and ordered a couple of beers. "Don't see either one of those yahoos in here," Mockingbird said. "Damn blizzard blowing like it is, ain't hardly no one in here." The barman brought the beer.

"Seen Jake James around?" Mike Duffy asked.

"Won't find him around Washoe City, Marshal. With Big Maude dead, you gotta know he's hightailed it for Virginia City or maybe even San Francisco. Think he run off with all her money? Word around town was that she had him on an allowance. Biggest loser I've ever met."

"I doubt he'd try to run in this blizzard," Mockingbird said.

"Whole town believes he killed Big Maude. Everybody's looking for the fool. If he's around, if he ain't run off like the dog he is, he'd be looking for the only man that's helped him in the past," the barman said.

"You talking about Frank Oberlin at the Lakeside Inn?" Mike Duffy stood back half a step. "Didn't think they were friends anymore."

"Jake ain't got any friends, Marshal. He uses people. Doesn't got a warm bone in him. Word is, he got out of jail, found his way here, and Oberlin took him in. That gentleman fed him, gave him work, and soon as Jake got a better offer, that is, to be Big Maude's husband, he run off on the man."

"Doubt if he'd try to go back now that Maude's dead," Mockingbird said.

"Might. Might need somewhere to wait out this storm. Particular if, as most here in town believe, he killed Maude. Like I said, man ain't got friend one." The barman walked off down the bar to talk with a couple of millworkers.

"Didn't ask him about Little Al," Duffy said.

"Little Al ain't welcome in most of the places around town. Caused too much trouble over the years." Mockingbird Jessup took a long drink of his beer. "I think I'd high-tail it to Parker Canyon and hole up in that cabin if I was Jake. If, as Bull and Slim believe, he has all that loot from the bank, he'd need a pack mule, and if he did head for the cabin, he's gonna be stuck there for a long time."

Duffy chuckled. "We're pretty much gonna be stuck, too, Sheriff. Is there any chance that Jake would return to Big Maude's Pleasure Palace to ride out this blizzard?"

"That is a thought, Marshal. Them women don't have much use for the man. He tried to lord it over them and Maude let him, sometimes. Without her to hold them in check, I don't think Jake would be safe at the whorehouse."

Mockingbird smiled at the thought of those girls ganging up on the man, beating the hell out of him, and tossing him out in the snow. "No, Duffy, I don't think we'll find him at Big Maude's."

The sheriff continued to chuckle, almost being able to see all those soiled doves whupping on old Jake James. He slapped the bar, finished his beer, and called for two more. He was trying to think where a man like Jake would hide. *He ain't got a friend, used 'em all up, has feed bags full of gold he can't spend.*

"He's got one big problem, Duffy. All that gold from the bank. He can't just run into some place and hunker down until the storm lifts. Somebody finds him with feed sacks full of gold, he's gonna die."

It was Duffy's turn to laugh. "Makes for an interesting picture, doesn't it? A lonely killer, afraid of his own shadow, looking to hide, yet dragging a couple of hundred pounds of gold with him. Seems to me he could just buy his way in somewhere."

"Of course!" Mockingbird yelped. "Damn right he could." He slapped Mike Duffy across the shoulders. "Good thinking, Marshal. Now, just where would that be that he could offer a piece of gold for a place to hide, be warm, maybe even get something to eat?"

"The man who helped him in the first place. Oberlin has a big heart. It might just kill him."

CHAPTER 18

"THERE AIN'T GONNA BE ANY KIND OF LET-UP IN THIS storm for at least another day," Mockingbird said. He and Duffy were at the stables saddling their horses. It would be just a short ride, less than two miles, to the Lakeside Inn, but through gale force winds driving tons of snow, they knew it would be a miserable ride.

"Marshal Service a little busy tonight," the smithy said. "You just missed that big angry sumbitch and his partner."

"Didn't happen to mention where they might be going, did they?"

"No, Mockingbird. No, they didn't, but, like you fellers, they ain't got a pack mule, ain't got no supplies, so it'd be my guess they're just going for a nice little mid-winter horseback ride around the lake."

Duffy chuckled as he finished buckling the girth strap for his horse. "Yup, Smithy, that's us. Just going for a nice little horsey ride. Ain't seen Jake James or Little Al Tyson by chance, have you?"

"Not since early this morning. Jake rented a mule

and horse and he ain't brought 'em back. Bastard best not of stole them critters. You find him, I want 'em back. Little Al had a large bundle and Jake had some sacks. That's a strange couple if you ask me. Ain't neither one worth a damn and dangerous as hell together."

Mockingbird moved over next to Duffy. "Pretty much cinches it, Marshal. He would have needed the pack mule for all that gold." He got a smile on his face. "Wonder if the big bundle he talked about was Big Maude? She was more than hefty but either one of those two could have carried her."

"My thoughts," Duffy said. "I was wondering what was in that bundle Little Al had? Remember, the girls said a big man helped Big Maude carry those feed sacks out and it wasn't Jake. Jake was outside holding the horses and mule. More and more I'm seeing Jake and Little Al all partnered up." Duffy looked over at the Smithy, wanted to ask more about that bundle but let it go. Was Big Maude in the bundle? Was she alive? How the hell do you even ask those questions?

"One thing, though," Duffy said. "If there was that third person, it almost had to Sweet Maria, even though she was the one told us about them."

"Most god-awful partnership I can think of," Mockingbird laughed. "We're only gonna find one of 'em alive, Marshal. You gotta know that." The sheriff turned to the smithy.

"Did you mention to the marshal what you just told us about Jake?"

"Didn't ask."

———

"You THINKING how easy it would be for a man to get lost in something like this?" Bull Morrison was leading the two for the short ride to the Lakeside Inn. "Can't see nothing." The snow was driven by strong gusty winds, swirling, stinging cheeks, blinding the eyes. Both men had shawls wrapped around their faces, hats pulled down as far as the ears would let them, and sat hunched over the saddle horns.

The sun had already dipped behind the crest of the Sierra Nevada and what would have been an early twilight became night. A deep, slightly gauzy darkness made staying on the road that much more difficult. "Don't want you hearing me bitch about the fog in San Francisco, Slim. This is far worse."

"Ain't the brightest two marshals in the service, are we?" Slim chuckled. "If it weren't for the edges of this road we wouldn't know we were on a road." They nudged their ponies up to the front of the Lakeside Inn and saw no lamps lit anywhere. Lamps would have given off a gauzy light through the driving snow and ice, creating almost moving shadows. They were looking at cold stone, areas of pitch black, and the only things moving were snowflakes being flung at their faces by gale force winds.

"Oberlin hibernatin', Slim? Let's get these critters out of the storm and see if we can roust the old Green Mountain Boy out without gettin' shot in the process. I don't think he'd be afraid of shootin'."

They walked around the building to where Slim had seen the corrals and weather stalls. "Somebody's here, Bull. A mule and a horse in that one corral. Wasn't here before. Best be careful, old man."

The animals tucked away, the two took a look in the

stall where the other animals were. "That mule had a pack saddle on him earlier today, Slim. Can still see the outlines. Somebody didn't even bother to brush him down."

"Don't see packs of any kind, either, Bull. No pack saddles, no canvas, no ropes. I'm afraid this animal came in packed and another animal rode out, packed. We ain't tried to be quiet, Bull, and ain't nobody bothered to find out who we are."

"We're not gonna like what we find inside that big building, Slim. I'll bet there are doors unlocked because of a hurried leave."

The two made their way through deep snow and strong wind to the front of the Lakeside Inn. Bull tried the door to the Lounge and found it locked but Slim opened the door to the restaurant and inn proper. "I can almost taste the danger," Slim said, stepping quickly inside. It was dark, no fires burning in the great stone fireplace, similar to the one in the lounge.

With the hazy twilight outside and the unlit interior, Slim couldn't see a thing. Anyone could be standing just inside that door with a knife, a gun, or a bludgeon, waiting for someone to step through. He pulled his Colt Army and cocked it before stepping through the doorway, didn't have time to let his eyes adjust, but stepped quickly into the interior and made a fast look all the way around. "Come on in, Bull. We're alone for the time being.

Bull strode up to the desk and lit a lamp, found another one and lit it as well. The large room was beautiful. Rock walls with rough timber holding up the ceiling and hanging groups of candle lit crystal chandeliers. Candle lit wall sconces and wrought iron displays on the walls made for a warm and friendly atmosphere. Half the room was where the reception desk was and chairs for those waiting spread around. Some near that centerpiece of a fireplace.

The other half appeared to be the dining area. Several large tables, seating four to six, were comfortably spaced around the area. "Kitchen must be back that way," Bull said. "Why don't you check it out and I'll see if anything's going on in the bar." He coughed. "Excuse me, the lounge."

Bull found the door connecting the Inn to the Lounge closed but not locked and opened it slowly. There was no reaction from inside and he slipped into the lounge, moved quickly to the unlit fireplace, and found a lamp. "Oh, damn, damn, damn," he said, easing down on his haunches after lighting the lamp. Frank Oberlin was crumpled in the area between the bar and the fireplace spread out in a pool of congealed blood.

"Got Oberlin," he called out to Slim and moved to take a close look. There was considerable blood but no indication of a fight or ruckus of any kind. No overturned chairs and tables, no broken glasses or bottles, and Oberlin's face wasn't bruised or bleeding. Bull rolled the man over after making sure he was still breathing and saw a nasty gash across the back of the man's head.

"Took a hell of a hit," Bull mumbled. He stepped behind the bar and found some bar rags to help stem the flow of blood and get the wound wrapped. *He needs a doc more than anything right now and I don't think we can move him. Means one of us is gonna have to make another horrible ride. Somebody just walked up to him and bashed his head in. Somebody he knew? Jake*

James maybe? Whoever it was won't like it when I catch him.

Bull Morrison looked around what he considered a fascinating room, seeing the incredible work that the man sprawled at his feet had done. *An artist in every sense of the word and gets his heads bashed in. By a friend? My mother was an artist.* The thought just popped into his head. He and his mother never really had a soft, friendly relationship. Bull was a bull even as a boy, and his mother wrote poetry, painted with water colors, and played piano.

My mother would be on her knees, sobbing softly, tending to those terrible wounds and I'm standing here with thoughts of killing the man who did this. She would never understand how empathetic I want to be at this very moment. Their artistry was different, but she would see his and he would see hers.

"Nobody in the kitchen," Slim said. He walked up and stood next to Bull Morrison. "He almost looks peaceful, doesn't he?" Slim Calhoun stepped behind the bar and found the cash box opened and empty. "Somebody wants us to believe this was a robbery."

"It was," Bull said. "Robbed this gentleman of his way of life." Slim had never seen Bull act this way. He appeared to be genuinely saddened by Oberlin's attack. "I never got close to the man like you did, Slim. When he was telling you about growing up in Vermont, about living in Inns and chalets like this, I could feel the man was real. There was nothing phony about Frank Oberlin. I'm sorry I wasn't able to know him like you did."

Bull seemed to be tired as he slowly got to his feet. "Don't want to think about what I want to do to the man who smashed his head like that." Finding Oberlin, as

Bull did, seemed to take the starch right out of the man and he moved to the fireplace and sat on the rock apron. He used a length of iron to stir the ashes. "This happened a long time ago, Slim. These ashes are cold." He crumpled some paper that was on the side of the apron along with kindling, built a small fire and added larger and larger chunks of split wood until he had a goodly fire blazing.

"One of us has to ride in for the doc, Slim. Oberlin ain't gonna live without solid medical treatment." He gave a sour look at Slim, knowing that it would probably be him making that ride. "We need this man alive to tell us what happened here."

Slim started to say something when they heard horses right outside the Inn's doors. Both men were on their feet, weapons in hand, racing for the reception area. "One move and you die," Slim said, finding two men stepping down from their saddles. "Step away from the horses, slowly, gentlemen. Slowly."

"It's us, Mike Duffy and Sheriff Jessup. Don't shoot, Slim." Mike Duffy held his arms well out to the side and stepped away from his horse. "Hopin' to find Jake out here."

Slim had to chuckle looking at the two. Scarves wrapped around their faces, hats pulled down tight, and both of them looking more like snow men than lawmen. He nodded to the two and slipped his big Colt back in its leather.

"Us, too," Bull said. "Come in, we got work to do."

They stretched Oberlin's body onto a settee near the fire, covered him with their own heavy coats, and tried to make the gentleman as comfortable as possible. The bleeding had been stemmed and he was breathing normally. The group then sat in chairs around the now fully lit fireplace. "We haven't been here that long," Bull said. "We know this part of the place is empty but haven't started going through the rooms."

"Whoever's responsible tried to make this attack look like a robbery," Slim said.

"Smithy told us Jake rented a horse and pack mule this morning. Didn't bother to tell you, he said." Duffy was looking at the fire as he talked. "Said Little Al was carrying a large bundle apparently either across the back of the saddle or on a mule. Smithy wasn't exactly giving out with the news."

"Believe that mule and horse are out there in the corral now," Slim said.

"Oberlin. He was a craftsman. Just look around this place," Bull said. He shook his head, trying to get his mind back on the business at hand. "There's a slightly worn pack mule in the corral out back, as Slim said, but no packs or bags of gold. Think Big Maude was in that bundle of Little Al's?"

"It seems that Jake may have brought the mule, gold, and Big Maude out here, got in a fight with Oberlin, and tried to kill him." Slim said. He found glasses and handed them around while Mockingbird found a bottle and poured for the group. "But what you said about Little Al being with Jake, I'm wondering."

"Maybe," Bull said. "Maybe it was Little Al that caved Oberlin's head in. It's for sure he and Jake were working together. We gotta get Oberlin to the doc's. We gotta search those rooms," he said, tossing down a hefty drink of good bourbon. "Mmm," he said. "Gonna miss this stuff." He walked toward the door to the reception area followed by the others. *Slim needs to tell me to calm down. I'm coming mighty close to getting riled.* He tried to smile at the thought.

"I'll ride for the doctor," Mockingbird Jessup said. "He'll respond faster to me than one of you, and I know my way around this old town even when you can't see." He had an ironic chuckle going as he headed out the door and into the tempest. Bull walked with him.

"Ride in nice and easy, Sheriff. This isn't the time to make mistakes. Keep your eyes as open as you can. We don't have any idea where either Jake or Little Al are. You're a good man, Mockingbird. This county's going to want to keep you around for a while."

"I know. I might seem old and worn out, but I'm still a thinking man. Thank you, Marshal."

CHAPTER 19

THE ENTRANCE TO THE HALLWAYS LEADING TO THE Lakeside Inn's rooms was a rock and rough-timber archway. Large Sierra Nevada slabs of granite were fitted into each other along with river rock and some exotic quartz. Bull pointed it out.

"That's rose quartz, Slim. Just look at that."

The whole archway was lined with rough cut timbers, stripped of their bark and almost polished after being placed. Wrought iron mounting finished off the entrance. The affect was that of a New England mountain hunting lodge. "Ain't never seen anything like this," Bull said.

The doors were heavy timber and the hinges were hand made of wrought iron as were the door handles. "More excellent work," Bull mused, pushing the double doors open with ease. Slim saw Bull stiffen up, saw a softer face harden quickly.

"You listen close now," Bull said. Slim knew he was back being a marshal. "If there's someone back here, he's already killed." He couldn't take his eyes off the beautiful rock, timber, and iron work. Slim saw him almost jerk his eyes away and again got his mind back on what they were doing.

"We know both Jake and Little Al rode out here. We know that Frank Oberlin was hit across the back of the head with something heavy and hard. And we know that only one person rode away from here. Either Jake or Little Al is back here in one of these rooms, maybe dead, maybe unconscious, or maybe waiting for one of us to open the door to his room. Got it?"

That's the way, Bull. I'm mighty glad you're back with us. Keep your anger under control and keep right on thinking, Slim's thoughts were on a positive note again. "I'm thinking, if someone moves and they're damn close, shoot 'em. If they're back a bit, try to subdue them, but always remember, either one of these men is a killer."

"And they're both big and strong. This ain't the time to play hero. Shoot the bastard," Bull said. He looked at Slim and Duffy and nodded. "Let's go hunting, boys."

There were two hallways, unlit, and Slim stepped quickly through the doors, his Colt in hand. The hallways had rooms off to one side only, and the hallways had one door that opened onto a court yard. The inn's reception and restaurant were the bottom third of a U.

"Duffy, you take those doors to the left. Each room opens to the outside, remember. Don't just assume there's no one about if you don't see someone. Bull, we'll go this way. It would be nice to take someone alive, if possible," he said.

Bull snorted. "Not likely. Somebody's gonna pay dearly for Frank Oberlin's bashed in head." *They terror-*

ized Big Maude. Beat the hell out of a decent man. Ain't no way I'm showing mercy to either one of those yahoos. Both need a fine whupping before they die.

Slim remembered what the outside of the building looked like, with a long porch running the length of each of the outside walls, so that individual rooms could open out to the open porch, or in to the hallway. The north porch faced the corrals with the starkly savage Sierra Nevada bulking so close while the south porch offered a view of Washoe Lake in better weather. Slim wondered if Oberlin actually got any spring and summer guests, or if he even cared. This inn was his dream.

That thought rolled around for some moments. Did Slim have a dream of a life after marshalling? Did he ever even think about such a thing? *That's a long way down the road, old sun.* But he knew at some point he would put the badge aside. What would happen after that? *Ain't got time for that kind of thinking.* But thoughts of a woman sharing part of his life, of children? He could see his arms around a lovely woman but could not get children to come into focus. *Get your mind back on the business at hand or sure as hell somebody's gonna bash your brains out.*

Slim stood next to the first room and listened for any kind of movement. Holding that big Colt, fully cocked, he slowly turned the door knob and eased the door open. Was someone standing close on the other side, holding an equally powerful weapon? Or maybe a knife? Or just a fireplace poker?

Slim glanced at Bull and pushed the door fully open, stepped in, and was eased aside by Bull making his entrance. The two marshals stood, guns ready and found the room empty. "One of three," Bull said. "Next one's mine."

Slim took the time to check the porch door and found it locked from the inside. He took a quick look under the bed, and into an open closet. "This one's clear," he said. "I'm going to get Duffy. He shouldn't be alone. I'll bring him back and the three of us will continue together."

"Good," is all Bull said. His mind was working over-time on a question he was going to wonder about for a long time. *If Jake and Little Al arrived here at some point why did only one leave? If the other didn't, why? That second man may very well be in one of these rooms but he'll surely be dead. My guess is we'll find Jake's body soon.* Bull had seen Little Al at that filthy saloon at the south end of the lake. Powerful, large, and sadistic, too. Bull wanted a shot at that man.

Bull walked out into the hallway and moved to the second room but planned on waiting for Duffy and Calhoun to join him. As he pressed an ear to the door he could hear thrashing inside the room. Grunts and thrashing is how he would explain it. He ran down the hallway and motioned for Duffy and Calhoun to hurry.

"Somebody's in there," he said, pointing at the door. "Somebody is alive."

Slim Calhoun could hear movement and slowly turned the knob, easing the door open. He didn't have time to make his move into the room. Bull and Duffy pushed their way through the doorway, guns drawn and stopped quickly. "So, we meet again," Bull said. "You don't look so good, Little Al. Something bothering you?"

Little Al Tyson was stretched out on the iron bedstead, flat on his back, his feet spread and tied to the iron bed posts, and his arms stretched and tied at the head of the bed. He had nasty cuts on his forehead, one ear ripped loose, and a crushed nose. The bleeding had drenched the mattress.

"The man was hit over and over with something heavy," Slim said. "Maybe that poker you used at the fireplace. Probably also used on Frank Oberlin. Little Al's lucky to be alive."

Little Al was still thrashing about to the point of almost overturning the bedstead. "Knock it off," Bull said. "You ain't dead yet but we could arrange it. Jake do this? Might have to give him a little more credit than I thought."

"We got a doctor coming, Tyson, so calm yourself or we will," Slim said. "That big ugly sumbitch is U.S. Marshal Bull Morrison. Me and Duffy there are Deputy U.S. Marshals, and you, sir, are under arrest. Specific charges will be explained in full, but for right now, murder. I know you can hear me, so, you want to talk about some of this?"

Little Al Tyson grunted, pulled and jerked on the ropes at both ends, but didn't say anything. "There is considerable money involved in all this, Tyson," Bull said. "I guess you thought some of it should be yours, eh?" Morrison used the barrel of his revolver to prod Tyson in the ribs, hard. Tyson's shirt had been all but ripped from his body and Bull was using red and blue bruises as targets for his prodding. "That was a question that needs an answer," he said and prodded again.

Tyson exploded with invectives, some of which Bull knew he would remember for future use. "That wasn't really an answer, Little Al. You can do better. Jake get off with all that money?" The end of the barrel was jammed into Tyson's ribs and the man yelled out.

"You damn right he did." Tyson was in great pain and Bull wasn't going to give him a chance to catch his breath.

Bull tried to smile and glanced up at Slim. "Who killed Big Maude? You?" He saw Tyson glaring at him through a face full of wet, sticky blood. The gun barrel prodded again, even harder. "Well?"

Tyson nodded and Bull got down in his face. "Couldn't hear you, Little Al," he said, and jammed the barrel hard into the ribs.

"Yes!" he yelled it out. The fury and hate boiled through eyes that told Bull Morrison there was also great pain in that huge body. It was a sickening sight and Slim Calhoun didn't hesitate to call Bull off. The man's skull had knots from several heavy blows, his nose was an open wound, bleeding and twisted off to one side. It was his ear that seemed out of place, ripped loose and just hanging by a little stretch of skin.

"We have our answers, Bull, and this man has suffered enough for one session." Slim looked in Al Tyson's eyes and saw pain. What he didn't see was a desire to help in the matter of finding Jake and the money from the bank robbery.

"Go get the chains, Slim. We'll chain his arms behind his back, chain his feet close together, and escort the gentleman into the lounge. We can wait for the doctor in the warmth of that fire." He prodded Little Al again. "And if you even so much as cough wrong, all three of us will shoot you dead."

Duffy moved around to the other side of the bed.

"Think he'll even be able to walk? He's taken some nasty blows to that thick skull of his."

"If we have to drag him, we will," Bull snorted. He was looking at Tyson's head, trying to understand how it was that Jake took the huge man down. *Must have waited for him to turn his back and slammed him hard, over and over. Would have been killer blows to anyone else. That tells me it was Jake who took out Frank Oberlin, too. Where is Jake? Where would he run to in a blizzard like what's blowing its horn right now?*

"Right now, Duffy, Jake is out there in this blizzard packing feed sacks full of gold and silver, and not a friend in the world. We might not find his body until spring thaw."

Little Al gasped, tried to say something, and Bull moved down next to him. "Go ahead, Tyson, spit it out. I'm listening."

"Parker Canyon," is all he said.

"Didn't need to hear that," Bull almost whispered. "Ain't no way in hell a man could make that ride in this weather." He looked up at Mike Duffy. "We ain't going, either. After the storm, maybe. That's a long-shot maybe."

Slim walked in dragging leg chains and holding the wrist chains. "That damn snow is coming down even harder, Bull. What's this about not going somewhere?"

"Seems Jake may be making a run for Parker Canyon and, old friend, we ain't gonna even make a try for it," Bull said and turned to Duffy. "Think that jail Mockingbird's got will hold Little Al?"

"It's strong, Bull. Rock, timber, heavy iron bars. It'll hold the fool. What are you thinking?"

"Need to get Frank Oberlin to the doc's and if the doc needs to treat Little Al, he can do it at the jail. We can chain the fool up so he can't hurt the doctor but we ain't putting him in a hospital or clinic. He's going to be behind bars until we arrange the hanging."

Little Al stumbled, bounced off the walls, fell twice, screaming the whole way. Some screams brought on by severe pain, some from severe anger. Leg irons allowed small steps, head injuries brought on his inability to keep his balance. And anger drove him to howl invectives at everyone and everything as they got him moved from the guest room to the lounge. He was flopped down on the floor near the fire. "Looks like Frank Oberlin is coming around, Slim," Duffy said. "That's a nasty wound."

Bull was first to Oberlin's side and settled on his haunches next to the settee. "You with us, Frank? This is Marshal Bull Morrison. Me and my deputy Slim Calhoun were out here earlier. We've got a doctor coming."

"Hurts," is all Oberlin said. His eyes opened for a moment and closed quickly. "I remember you," he coughed, spraying some blood. "Ribs. Hurt."

Slim had never seen this gentle, caring attitude in Bull Morrison. They'd been partners in this law enforcement life of theirs for several years, broken up major gangs of outlaws, sent many men to lonesome and cold graves. For Bull Morrison to show empathy and caring like this was a sight to see. *There's something very different about Frank Oberlin to bring these kinds of feelings from the grouchy old marshal. Is it the craft of building this place? I hope I find out.*

If he asked, Bull wouldn't be able to give an answer. Was it that Oberlin made him think of his mother? Doubtful. Was it that Morrison was giving thought to what his life would be like if he hung up his badge? Even more doubtful. Bull would not answer the question simply because he didn't know.

Bull eased the man so that he was closer to flat on his back. "That help? Didn't know you had broken ribs, too." Bull motioned for Slim to help get the man's shirt off. "Damn, damn," Bull said. The bruises were stark on the man's pale skin, and the distinct marks of that fireplace poker stood out. Bull Morrison had to shake his head as he found himself looking at his mother, not Frank Oberlin.

These two people, his mother from so many years ago, and Frank Oberlin, a friend from yesterday, were alive in Bull's mind, rendered helpless by thieving outlaws, beaten unmercifully, and left to rot. They were creative people, alive with beauty, seeing the harmony offered by nature, and left to rot as a piece of trash might be. No one saw Bull Morrison take a swipe across his face.

"Hear horses," Duffy said. He pulled his weapon and motioned for Slim to join him as a welcoming committee at the front door. The doctor was trying to get blankets moved off him so he could climb down from the wagon and Mockingbird was tying off the team.

Slim stepped out into the maelstrom to help the doctor and grabbed up the blankets. "Thank you. Am I too late?"

"No, but now you have two patients, one of whom is in chains."

"My lord," he said, following the marshals and the sheriff into the Lakeside Inn. "What happened out here?" He glared at Bull Morrison as if to say, "What have you done?" The look was returned in kind.

"I'm Doctor Elroy, James Elroy. What happened?"

Slim saw the look on Bull's face and stepped in quickly. "Frank Oberlin was attacked by, we think, Jake James. He also attacked this man, Little Al Tyson. Both men are in extreme pain, Doctor. It would be best to start with Frank Oberlin. Tyson can wait."

"I'll need fresh warm water and some clean linen." He kneeled down near Oberlin, opened his medical bag, and started making an assessment of the damage done to the man. "What was used to do this kind of damage?"

"Think it might have been the fireplace poker," Bull said. "You make this man well. He's a fine craftsman, a gentleman, and…" Bull choked up some. He coughed to hide it, and stepped back as Duffy brought a hand full of linen napkins from the dining room.

"Water'll be here shortly," he said.

Doctor Elroy snuffed quietly and looked around the room. "Keep that fire going and be prepared to keep bowls of warm water coming as well. If you plan on holding conversations, I'd be pleased if you do it elsewhere. I'll call if I need anything."

Bull motioned everyone into the reception and dining area, away from Doc Elroy. "Crusty old bastard, ain't he?" he said, chuckling softly. "I'd love to punch that arrogant little face of his."

"Wait until everyone's healed up, Bull." Slim added some wood to the fire in the dining room. "Anybody made coffee yet?"

"Hope so," Bull said. "At least I remembered to bring this little bottle of bourbon."

Duffy headed immediately toward the kitchen. "Coming up," he said.

CHAPTER 20

IT WAS A MONUMENTAL EFFORT MOVING THE WOUNDED Frank Oberlin and Little Al Tyson from the Lakeside Inn. First stop was Doctor Elroy's hospital to leave Oberlin and then to the jail to lock up Tyson. Slim Calhoun chuckled remembering just how difficult that long night had become. They moved Tyson to the wagon first and chained him tight before getting Oberlin wrapped in blankets out. The wind never let up and the snow continued building high drifts, hiding features that were needed to navigate back to town.

There were features that had to be avoided or evaded, as well, such as ditches alongside the road that couldn't be seen and unseen potholes that could rip a wheel right off the wagon. Mockingbird drove the wagon, his horse tied to the back, and for the long ride the air was split, sundered, by Little Al Tyson's use of the language of the gutter.

Little Al thrashed about in the bed of the wagon constantly, trying to kick Frank Oberlin, trying to bite the doctor, threatening death to everyone involved.

Duffy tied his horse to the back of the wagon and rode with the doctor sitting next to him. "I'd like to silence the man, Doctor, but that wouldn't be proper for a Marshal. It's gonna be long ride, I'm afraid." The attempt at humor went right over the doc's head.

"Did you men have to beat him so badly? Seems to me you've already exceeded your authority."

Duffy chuckled, looking the doctor right in the eye. "We ain't touched the fool. We're almost certain that this was the work of Jake James. It's a long story, Doc. Goes all the way back to that gruesome set of killings up Parker Canyon and the bank robbery before."

"As badly as Tyson's hurt I don't want him in my hospital," Doctor Elroy said. "Frank Oberlin needs to be there but not that brute."

"We'll leave you and Oberlin off and the get Tyson locked up. You'll have to do your doctoring in his cell but one or two of us will be right with you." It took just a moment and Doctor Elroy nodded his acceptance, as if that was needed.

The storm had no desire to let up and the two mile drive to the doctor's hospital took a long time. Getting Frank Oberlin in was not difficult and Mockingbird then drove the wagon to the county complex and the Washoe County jail.

"Only good thing about this," Mockingbird said, "is the cells are on the first floor. We should be able to hustle this character right in."

Unfortunately, Little Al Tyson had other plans and simply went limp, would not cooperate in the least. Slim wrapped a line around one foot and Bull Morrison did the other, and they dragged Little Al across the storm ravaged courthouse yard, plowing a grand furrow in the snow. Then, it was up the stone steps, down the hall, through the office, and they laid him out on the floor of a cell. "Don't think the doc would have approved of that, either," Duffy laughed.

Tyson was in no condition to fight the marshals as they unlocked the leg irons and the wrist chains, and left him on the floor. "There's a blanket on the bed, tough guy," Bull said, slamming the cell door and locking it. "Breakfast later, supper later still. The judge will be in town in a few days, maybe. Have yourself a grand day."

"I think it's my turn to eat a bear," Slim Calhoun said. "He's about as heavy as one. Hope Uncle Bob's is open." They stood on the steps to the courthouse seeing the first shreds of light over the crest of the Virginia Range. "Ain't the kind of night I want on a regular basis."

––––––––

Silas Thompson lived alone above his apothecary just a block off the main street in Washoe City. He was spartan, lived as simply as a man could, eating lightly of meat and what few vegetables could be found midwinter. He was not known to fish or hunt. His little apartment had a door that opened to a stairway that led down to his store, and a door that opened to stairs that led down to an alley between buildings. Both doors locked from the inside.

Thompson was a reed of a man, standing almost six feet tall but as skinny as the smallest willow twig. He received his apothecary knowledge during the great war and moved west as the great war continued. The war raged in the east, and his broken body was mustered out before it gave up. He vowed he would only help, never hurt another human being. He was among the few men in Nevada Territory who didn't own a single weapon of any kind.

The heavy winter storms had brought on a rash of sore throats, colds, coughs, and the dreaded flu, too. He had been one of the busiest men in town because of it. Even late at night, when all the lamps in the building had been shut off, people banged on the door of the apothecary. He was not the kind of man who would turn his back on someone needing his services.

"Coming. I'm coming." He made his way down the stairs and into his little store, frigid at this late hour. He found his lamp near the counter, got it lit, and walked to the storefront door, fumbled with keys and the lamp, and finally got the door opened. "Jake? Is that you, Jake James?"

"I need help, Silas. In bad need of help." Jake wasn't wearing a heavy coat despite the wild tempest coursing through Washoe Valley; in fact, even his shirt was ripped half off. His head was bleeding, his face was scratched and cut, bleeding profusely, and he needed help getting inside the small store.

Thompson helped him in, got him in a chair, and got the front door closed. The long thin man knew he would be unable to help Jake up those steep stairs and instead worked to quickly get a fire going in the pot-belly near the counter. He couldn't help seeing the thin layer of ice on the inside of his front window.

Seeing someone as badly hurt as Jake brought back scenes from Virginia, scenes of badly wounded men, some in blue, some in gray, all needing his help. He wore blue, supported Lincoln and the Union, but would never not help another human being.

Jake James was not the kind of man Silas Thompson would be associated with, but he was a man and he needed help. "Let's see what we can do, here, Jake. Was it a bear or a cougar that attacked you?"

Jake didn't have the strength even to chuckle at the comment and just sat slumped in the chair as Silas got coffee boiling and water warming. He stripped what was left of Jake's shirt and wrapped a wool point blanket around the wounded man and started cleaning the head wounds first. "What on earth happened?"

"Don't rightly know," Jake said. He was having a hard time focusing, felt more like sleeping than talking, and Silas kept on cleaning him up. *Jake ain't the nicest man I've ever known, don't much care for his way of like or those he's associated with, but these wounds are horrible. He was attacked by more than one person and hit with different weapons.*

Silas Thompson spent a couple of hours cleaning and dressing the many wounds, keeping the fire going, making more than one pot of coffee, and watched as the light of day slowly transformed his view outside the door. *Sunrise? My God what a mess we have here. I need to get word to Big Maude that Jake's alive and that she needs to get him moved back to their place.* He was not aware of the previous activities around Washoe City, being busy tending to others.

He managed to get Jake moved to a settee that he shoved over close to the stove. Jake's legs and feet hung over an arm but he was on his back covered in two warm blankets. The man slept like a baby after being given a stiff dose of laudanum. Silas Thompson went upstairs to his apartment, got the fires lit and had a quick breakfast of side meat and a slice of bread he'd baked the day before.

Getting back downstairs, Thompson was trying to figure out what to do. The storm was still howling. Snow blowing in every direction as the winds tore through the streets of the busy little village. *Big Maude needs to know about this, and I think Mockingbird does too. I don't want to be seen going into that whore house, though.*

He fed the fire, got it blazing good and knew it would be fine for an hour or so, put on a sweater and heavy coat, grabbed his hat, and headed the three blocks to the sheriff's office. Just a stick of a man, he was having a terrible time negotiating heavy drifts, some as much as much as three feet deep, ice so slick he felt he was skating more than walking, and fighting that demon wind.

He was exhausted, and as he passed by Uncle Bob's Café, he spotted Mockingbird having breakfast with three men. It was a fight and he managed to get inside and get the door closed. "I need help, Jessup," he said, sliding into a chair, physically drained, all but helpless. He fumbled with a cup of coffee shoved in front of him.

"Silas," Mockingbird said. "What the hell happened to you?"

Thompson noticed that the four men appeared as tired and worn out as he felt. "It's Jake James, Big Maude's so-called husband, Sheriff. He's at my place and in terrible condition. Somebody needs to let Big Maude know and I won't go into her place. Might I ask why you men look almost as bad as Jake, just not bleeding?"

"Who is this man?" Bull Morrison growled.

"This is our apothecary, Marshal," Mockingbird said. "Silas Thompson, say hello to Marshals Morrison, Calhoun, and Duffy." Jessup looked at Thompson and shook his head. "I guess you haven't heard. Big Maude was murdered and we've been looking for Jake. What happened to him?"

"I swear it looks like he got in a fight with a mountain lion. Covered in cuts, scratches, and bruises. Some of his wounds are serious and some just scratches. He's in bad shape, Sheriff." Thompson looked around the table, nodded to each of the marshals. "I didn't know about Big Maude. What happened?"

"That's what we want to talk to Jake about," Slim said. "Did he say anything to you?"

"Only that he needed help," Thompson said.

"I don't suppose he was packing some heavy feed bags?" Bull said, just the slightest smile across his normally angry face. "I think we better go visit the man, maybe move him in with Little Al."

CHAPTER 21

"I NEED TO GET BACK TO THE OFFICE," MOCKINGBIRD Jessup said as the group finished their breakfast and was about to escort Silas Thompson back to his shop. "Who knows how much damage Tyson has done."

"We'll keep you informed," Slim said. It was full daylight, minus the cloud cover, as they made their way to the apothecary. "Jake say anything at all?" Slim asked.

"About what happened? No. He seemed reticent to discuss the situation," Thompson said. "Whatever it was that attacked him, it almost succeeded in killing him." Thompson fumbled with the lock on the door, finally getting it open, probably just before Bull Morrison would have kicked it in.

Jake James was still spread out on the settee by the big stove and while Thompson fed the stove, Morrison poked the man awake. "Sit up, Jake. I'm U.S. Marshal Bull Morrison and I've got some questions for you. Sit up, damn it." Bull poked him harder.

"Marshal? What?" Jake was still in his drugged up dream world and was fighting the pokes, the cloudy mind, and the awkward position he was in on the settee. He finally swung his legs around and came up to a sitting position, holding his throbbing head. "Oh, damn, that hurts." He looked around at Bull and Slim. "Marshal? I don't understand."

"The hell you don't," Bull said. "Can you get us some coffee, Mr. Thompson. This might take some time. Keep that stove hot, too, please." He shucked his heavy jacket, and pulled a chair over next to the settee. "Now, Jake, we've got a long talk in front of us. First off, what happened here?"

Slim pulled a second chair up while Silas put together a pot of coffee. "You've been mauled, Jake, and it isn't likely that it was a wild animal that did the damage." Bull listened to his partner but was having a hard time holding his anger. "Better start talking while you have the chance because if my partner gets himself all riled up, you'll really understand the meaning of the word mauled. Tell us what happened."

Jake sat quiet, looked first at Bull and then at Slim, but didn't say a word. Bull reached out and with an open hand, slapped the injured man across the side of his head. "We don't much care for your attitude, Jake. Start talking or it's off to jail with you."

"Jail? It ain't illegal to get beat up," Jake cried softly. Blood from numerous wounds was showing through Silas Thompson's bandages.

"Who beat you up?" Bull demanded, that big open palm just itching for another shot at Jake's head.

Jake couldn't keep his eyes off the open hand, but still, he just sat there, not saying a word. "Better take over, Slim, before I put a serious hurt on this fool." Bull got up and stood next to the stove, the anger evident in his face and attitude. "Gets the hell beat out of him and too dumb to tell us who did it."

Bull took the coffee offered by the apothecary, nodded, and kept on talking. "We've got a whole string of dead people, Jake, and we got us a pretty good idea that you're responsible."

"I'm wondering where those big sacks of plunder are, too." Slim moved to stand off to the side of Jake. "Probably got them stole, you think?" Slim looked over at Bull, a sly smile played across his face. "And he doesn't want to talk about it. Probably knows full well who stole those dirty old feed sacks he's been carrying around." Slim had a half grin on his face, and could see what he was saying had Jake's attention.

"Here's the way I see it," Bull said, back in full control. "Big Maude had all that bank loot and Jake wanted it. So did Little Al Tyson. So, Jake, you killed Big Maude and you and Tyson made off with the loot. Then, you tried to kill Tyson and ran off with the loot yourself, only to have it stole right out of your greedy hands." Bull looked at Slim.

"How'm I doing, Slim? Sound logical to you?" Bull had a satisfied look on his face and glared at Jake James.

"Sounds damn reasonable to me," Duffy said. He'd been standing off to the side watching Bull's little show. "Lots of gold missing from this picture."

"I think you're right as hell," Slim Calhoun said. He got in Jake's face. "Where are those sacks, Jake? Did you lose them? Or did some big bad outlaw beat you half to death and take them from you? Best answer that question pretty damn soon."

Bull saw the change in Jake's face and attitude and nodded gently. "Thank you, Jake," he said.

"Didn't say anything," Jake said.

"Didn't have to, dummy. Your body language told me everything I need to know." Bull laughed, stood up fast and took a long stride toward Jake who almost jumped back off the settee. The move was painful enough for Jake to whimper. "Ain't gonna hit you, Jake. Sure do want to, for the way you treated your dear departed wife, but right now I just want to ask who it was beat the hell out of you and stole all that bank loot? Best start answering these questions."

"I don't know what you're talking about," Jake said. "I didn't rob no bank."

"Time to put this gentleman behind bars, Slim."

"Yup. Simple charges. Attempted murder of Frank Oberlin, attempted murder of Little Al Tyson, murder of Maude James. That'll keep him off the streets for a long time."

"You're forgetting the murder of the sheriff and his deputy. The murder of the two ranch hands, and the murder of Crazy Ned and his gang of bank robbers," Bull Morrison said. "Add all them murders and attempted murders up and we'll have to hang old Jake James two or three times to eke out proper justice."

Slim and Duffy were laughing loud and hard when Bull got through. He looked at Jake. "You getting the picture, dummy? Who beat you up?"

Jake sat quiet, didn't move, wouldn't look at anyone in the store. "Okay then," Slim said. "Let's get him behind bars."

"He's wounded bad," Silas Thompson said. "He can't go to jail in that condition. It isn't right."

"The man he'll be in jail with is in worse shape, Mr. Thompson, and his wounds came by way of Jake.

Doctor Elroy will now have two patients to care for." Slim had a nasty smile on his face.

"Think we should put Jake in the same cell as Little Al?" There was a gasp and a long wail and Slim said, "Probably not, eh?"

"You almost killed Frank Oberlin, Jake, and you came up short on Little Al as well. Tyson is in our little jail and we only have the one cell."

Silas Thompson said, quickly, "No, Marshal. No. There are three cells there. I know, I've had to bring medicine to the sheriff."

Bull spun and knew his little game went south on him. "Damn, Mr. Thompson, I guess you're right." He had a hard time keeping from smashing the drug peddling apothecary, looked at Slim who had to turn away, and went back to Jake.

"We have Tyson in jail, Jake, charged with the murder of Big Maude. You'll be charged with that crime and all the others my partner outlined a few minutes ago. We're going to track down that bank loot, Jake, and maybe come up with even more charges to throw at you. For the time being, you'll be in a cell next to Tyson. I wouldn't get too close to those bars separating you. He has long arms."

Silas Thompson started to say something and Slim shushed him immediately, knowing he was going to remind Bull that he could put Jake in the third cell and keep the two well apart. That would have been the wrong thing to have said.

CHAPTER 22

"I DONE WHAT YOU TOLD ME, JAKE. MOVED THE PACKS onto the other mule. You still want me to hide all that at Big Maude's?" Sweet Maria gave the big outlaw a smile. "Some of the girls ain't gonna like this."

It wasn't a case of the doves not liking Jake, more often it was a case of hatred. He couldn't keep his hands off, wouldn't take no for an answer, had no respect for anything or anyone. Sweet Maria was one of the few who tolerated the man, and at this moment, she had control of thousands of dollars that Jake thought was his and his alone.

Sweet Maria tolerated Little Al Tyson as well, and learned from him that he and Jake were going to murder Big Maude and make off with the gold from the bank robbery. Tyson said they needed a third person to move the loot since the law would surely come looking for he and Jake. Sweet Maria became a part of the plan. Jake didn't know the whole plan, however.

"Those girls won't like you hiding out there."

"I know," Jake said. "This storm wasn't in the plan.

Ain't nothing we can do about it, though. Can't run off like we planned with this storm keeping us tied down."

Sweet Maria smiled, thinking of that plan. "I was looking forward to that long ride to San Francisco with you. Just you and me, the pack animals, and long days in the saddle. This storm should break up in a couple of days. Then we can go."

Sweet Maria smiled to herself. Her plan wasn't what she talked about. Her plan included Little Al.

Then I can go, Jake said to himself. *Nobody but me is making that ride.* "You get back to Maude's while you can, get those packs stored in the wood shack, and I'll join you as soon as I take care of Little Al." *He still thinks I'm bringing those sacks in to split with him. Only thing I'm bringing to that room is a fireplace poker and the only split-ting will be his big head.*

Sweet Maria wrapped her arms around the big man, kissed him long and wet, and let his hands roam where he wished. "Hurry off now. I'll be there in just a couple of hours." He watched her all the way to where she had the horse and mule tied and went back into the Lake-side Inn to finish his business with Frank Oberlin first and then Little Al.

It wasn't a pleasant ride back into town but with the storm, she wasn't seen by many. The snow was falling softly not being driven quite so hard. The gale winds would come up soon. Getting the packs unloaded at the wood shack and stored out of the storm was nowhere near the trouble it had been loading the heavy sacks. She moved the animals under a storm shed in the Plea-sure Palace corrals, and made her way into the building by way of the back steps and into the kitchen.

"Where have you been?" Naomi asked. She was at

the large kitchen table clutching a steaming cup of coffee.

"Hot coffee," Sweet Maria said, grabbing a cup and reaching for the pot. "Oh, that's good." She sipped the steaming brew and settled down at the table. "Had some business to take care of," she said. "Ran into Jake. He swears it wasn't him that killed Big Maude. He feels terrible, wants to come back here, run the place like Maude did."

"Them marshals said he probably does own the place," Naomi said, "but I don't want that creep around here, wanting what I sell, grabbing stuff thats for sale. Man's a creep."

"It ain't gonna be our choice," Sweet Maria said, drinking more of the coffee.

"We'll see about that." Naomi walked out of the kitchen to find the other girls. It was still the middle of the afternoon and there weren't any customers what with the storm getting stronger and louder, bashing its way into Washoe Valley.

"He puts his hands on me one more time and I'll break his arm," one of the girls said when Naomi brought the news.

"I'll kill the bastard," another said. There were five women working at Big Maude's Pleasure Palace and four of them agreed that Jake would not be welcomed. The threats varied from scratching his eyes out to plunging a carving knife in his heart. That came from Naomi, and she smiled saying it.

———

JAKE HAD his ugly business with Frank Oberlin done and walked back to where Little Al was waiting. "Got those packs coming our way, Tyson. big storm coming in so we'll get this split and get the hell out of here."

He had wiped the blood from the fireplace poker and had it hidden under his big buffalo robe coat, waiting now for the right time to attack Little Al Tyson. "Shouldn't a brought that whore into this, Jake. Now, she knows too much. Best to kill her off soon." He had been standing near the door that led outside, turned and walked to the window.

When Tyson moved the curtains aside to look out the window, Jake attacked. He slammed the poker into Little Al's head, three, four times, then whipping it into the big man's ribs, his kidneys, and then back to his head. Tyson was a giant of a man but no man could withstand Jake's attack. It was more than vicious, and Little Al slowly sank to the blood covered stone floor. Jake hit the unconscious outlaw twice more just to be sure and dragged him to the bed.

It was a circus getting him up and onto the mattress, but getting him tied securely was far easier. "Somebody's gonna find these bodies and they are gonna want to know what brought all this on," Jake mused. He went into the lounge, wiped the poker somewhat clean, found Oberlin's money box and emptied it. "That's a good reason."

————

THE RIDE into Washoe City was difficult. The storm had increased in intensity, winds driving ice crystals and snow at gale force, vision limited, and the going slow. He rode right up to the corral, saw the mule and horse Sweet Maria brought in, smiled, and walked to the kitchen door. *I'll be safe here for a few days, which will give me time to do a little more planning. As soon as the storm lets up, I'll let Maria think she's coming with me, dump her somewhere between here and Lake's Crossing, and make my way to Denver.*

Jake had let Sweet Maria believe they were going to San Francisco so if she did mention it to anyone, the law might look for him there. Denver was where he wanted to be, and this time, he would run the whore house his way. It would be plush, lots of velvet, beautiful young girls, the finest liquor, and nobody got in free.

He'd had that dream ever since the first day in prison. There were two dreams. Kill Singing Sammy and own a whorehouse. Singing Sammy was dead, and Jake smiled at the thought, but Big Maude's was not the whorehouse of his dreams. The one in Denver would be. "Little Al should have used his head. Somebody's gonna figure out who killed Maude and fingers are gonna point right at me. Could have done it better. Tyson's just a bull."

He walked into the kitchen with a smile on his face, those good thoughts of Denver still working their way through his head. "Afternoon, girls," he said, finding three of them around the stove. The attack was brutal and swift. There were knives, scissors, fire wood, ax handles, and knuckles and feet involved. Jake never saw it coming, was unable to defend himself, and was whipped and beaten on for several minutes.

Blood was spattered on the girls, kitchen floor and walls, and flowed from multiple wounds. Anger that had built over time was flushed free and the girls found it hard to stop the brutal beating. Some smashed the helpless man because of how he treated them while other's anger was from the horrible death of Big Maude. Regardless of why, the what was sickening to look at.

Jake James, once the half-owner of this busy little whorehouse, was crying out in pain, sobbing actually, his head bleeding from numerous bashings, his arms hit with everything that could be swung, sliced with every sharp object that could be found, and finally the outlaw just fell to the floor.

Naomi called the attack off when there was no response from the man. "He's unconscious, girls. Let's just roll him out the door and off the porch."

"I think we ought to make sure he's dead," one of them said.

"He'll be dead laying out there in the storm. Be sunset in an hour. Somebody will find his body under a snow drift in a day or two."

Sweet Maria was horrified at what she saw but then she came to realize just what it meant. It meant that Sweet Maria was one rich bitch, and the smile lit up the hallway between the kitchen and the front room of Big Maude's Pleasure Palace. "I'll be out of here as soon as this storm is over," she muttered softly. She went to her room to do some serious planning. "Gotta be twenty thousand dollars or more out there. Little Al will be waiting."

———

"THIS MAN HAS BEEN HORRIBLY ATTACKED, Marshal Morrison. I don't understand how a man of your position could do this to another human being." Doctor

James Elroy was standing outside the cell where Jake was being held. Jake was whimpering, wrapped in a fetal position under two wool point blankets. "I just don't understand."

"Ain't nothing to understand, Doc," Bull said, doing his best to give the good doctor a big smile. "Ain't none of us did this. This is how he was found by Silas Thompson, so let your mind be at ease and get him healed up so we can hang the bastard."

"Humph," is all the response Bull got back and Doc Elroy left the jail. Bull snickered some and made his way to the office and a warm stove, a tin cup half filled with coffee, the other half with decent bourbon.

"All we gotta do now is find the loot, find whoever did the beating, and make sure we know who did all the killing. Just another day in the life of someone in the Marshal Service, eh Slim?"

"It is so," Slim laughed. "Someone rode out of the Lakeside Inn leading a mule laden with thousands of dollars in stolen gold. That's our first job. Find that person."

"Not in this storm, we ain't," Duffy said. "I vote for a good long talk-it-over session at The Timbers."

The sheriff and three marshals agreed and they fought their way through the blizzard toward the friendly saloon, talking the entire way. "At least Doc Elroy said that Frank Oberlin was going to pull through. I want to get to know that man," Bull said.

"He's going to be able to tell us a lot of what we need to hear," Slim said. Slim looked at his partner and couldn't get the idea of a change in the man out of his head. It was such a dramatic change when he talked about or even to Frank Oberlin. Bull Morrison, the man who destroyed saloons on a good day, has captured or killed more outlaws than any other in the marshal service, has a complete change of personality when Oberlin's name comes up.

Is it possible that Bull Morrison had dreams of building something such as Oberlin has built? Is Bull Morrison a craftsman at heart, not a gun toting lawman? Is there something in the art of architecture that has such a pull on this man? Slim Calhoun has ridden as his partner for years and has never seen such an attitude change. He wrenched himself from these thoughts and got back on the problem at hand.

"This idea of a third person bothers me. We had Jake just about pinned for the Parker Canyon massacre, and Little Al figured for Maude's death, and now, out of the blue, we have a third person loaded down with thousands of dollars of bank loot and whorehouse funds."

"There are three seriously wounded men who might be able to tell us if they live through their ordeal," Bull said.

"Think Jake might be tied up with one of the working girls?" Duffy asked.

"From what we heard, they hated the man," Slim said.

"Seems the wind is back down to gale force from hurricane," Mockingbird said. "I can actually see across the street. See? Ain't a soul walking the streets but us fools."

The four tied off their tired and ice covered horses and made their way through deep drifts and through the swinging batwing doors at The Timbers. The place was almost empty. "In most places, storms are usually good for the bar business," Slim said. "Guess that ain't so in Washoe City."

"Even the mills are closed," the barman said. "I've sold more coffee than demon rum today," he laughed. "What can I get you fellers?"

"Ain't gonna be coffee," Bull snorted. "Give us a bottle and glasses and then bring us big steins of beer." Bull took the bottle, Slim grabbed the glasses, and they found a table close to the fire roaring in the rock fireplace.

"Looks like a fine place to set up camp," Mockingbird said. "All the comforts of home."

"'Cept one," Duffy said.

"And just what is missing?" Bull said. He poured drinks for them and watched the barman set flagons of beer on the table.

"She should be warm and willing," Duffy laughed.

"We could have this meeting at Big Maude's Pleasure Palace," Mockingbird laughed. He stopped, looked around the table. "You know, gentlemen, that might not be that bad an idea. The condition that Jake is in, that fool might have tried to go back there."

It was quiet for several seconds, the men looking back and forth, taking in all the possibilities of what the sheriff said, shaking their heads. Bull broke the silence. "Mockingbird, you are right as rain, but we need to sit here for an hour, enjoy this bottle, and talk freely. We must visit Maude's though." He sat back, felt the heat from the fireplace mingling with the heat from the whiskey, and actually got a full smile across his face.

"He's right," Slim said. "We have a generous supply of questions that need to be answered, more than enough wounded and injured people whose current status needs to be questioned, and far too many dead people. In my opinion most of the answers can be found from the two men in Mockingbird's jail. The rest can be found at Maude's. The men in jail are in no condition to be grilled."

"Oberlin will know something, too, but like Jake and Little Al, he ain't ready to be hammered with questions." Sheriff Mockingbird Jessup looked into the fire, settled back in his chair, and thought about Frank Oberlin, Jake James, and Little Al Tyson. "Those three wounded men have all of our answers, gentlemen. They know everything that we're trying to learn about."

The table got quiet as the men took in what Mockingbird just said and the irony of the entire situation. Four seasoned lawmen with multiple murders, large sums of stolen money, and intrigue by the gross, and it was three seriously wounded men who couldn't talk who had the answers.

"After we're warmed and comfortable, our questions known, and maybe even one or two answered, we'll head for Maude's," Bull said. There were two women who did most of the talking when they first were there. Naomi and Sweet Maria. Those two would be the first to be questioned.

"I don't think we should walk in with pre-gone conclusions, either," Slim said. "We might believe it was the whores who whipped the daylights out of Jake but we should be open to other possibilities. There is that third person and we can't assume that third person is one of the whores. As reasonable as it seems," he chuckled.

"You should stay with the prisoners, Mockingbird," Bull said, "unless you've already hired a jailer."

"Ain't even had time to change my socks much less hire someone. Don't want to, but you're right. Somebody has to stay with those two." He had a wry grin on his face thinking how much fun it would be to watch Bull Morrison question the five girls at Big Maude's Pleasure Palace.

CHAPTER 23

"Looks like our storm might be breaking up some," Duffy said as the three walked out of the saloon. Snow was slowly cascading in its simple ballet, not being urged on by strong winds. There was the slightest hint of sunshine filtered somewhat by dissipating clouds, and even a few people were venturing out.

"It's gonna be a nice day after all," Duffy said. Steam engines were thumping, making their presence known, a few storekeepers were trying to shovel snow off the boardwalks, and more than one of the drayage companies were using large sleds or sleighs to make their rounds.

The snow drifts were difficult to move through but the lack of wind did help. "I'd like you, Slim to spend some time going through some of the outbuildings when we get to Maude's."

Bull Morrison said. "If our third person is one of Maude's girls, we might just get lucky and find the bank loot."

"Hard to think she would bring it back but, really,

where else would she go?" Slim looked at the other two. "Someone has all the gold, and with the weather changing, it might be possible to leave town but it sure would leave an obvious trail."

"Where would you go?" Duffy was kicking his way through a drift right on the wooden sidewalk. "North or south, the roads would be fierce."

"The idea of running away with more than twenty thousand dollars is pretty good incentive," Bull snorted.

During the hour long session at The Timbers, the idea of a third person became more and more obvious. Jake doing the killing at Parker Canyon, Jake and Little Al killing Big Maude and ripping off the bank loot, and now, a third person working with Jake to take the bank loot and hide it at Maude's. All conjecture, but more than possible.

"I think I saw at least three, maybe four structures of some kind. Near the corrals, near the back porch." Slim said. "There's a back door off the kitchen and one or more of the girls could scoot out and grab the money and run."

"Not in what this storm dropped on us," Mockingbird laughed. "Unless they had a team and sleigh."

"Bingo!" Duffy smiled. "Perfect, and we've seen our share of sleighs in the last few hours."

That thought occupied their minds during the two block walk to Big Maude's. Even though the wind had become a light breeze, the air was frigid. Ice formed around nostrils, hung from beards and hair, and the men were ready for a long session near the fireplace in the confines of the gaudy whore house.

"Might want to keep that in mind, Slim," Bull chuckled. "We've seen more than one sleigh since we got here.

Whoever ran off with that loot took the horse and mule, too."

Sure did, Slim thought. *If I had all that money, a team and a sleigh, where would I go? Lake's Crossing, fifteen or so miles north would give me access to the emigrant trail east and west. San Francisco or Denver? Carson City, ten miles or so south would give me access to the other emigrant trail. Or, does our third person already have a place close by where she could hide comfortably until spring?*

The walkway to the Pleasure Palace porch had not been shoveled nor had the steps up to the door. "I'll bet a dollar that would have been one of Jake's duties," Slim laughed and made his way around the building leaving Bull and Duffy to fight their way up the steps. The door was unlocked, of course and the marshals walked into the warm reception area.

Naomi was putting a log on the fire and turned with a smile, hoping the men were customers. There had been few because of the storm and because of the death of Big Maude. "Oh, it's you," she said. She scowled and jabbed the log hard with a poker. "Hoping you were customers. You here to cause more trouble?"

"That's my business," Bull said, giving Duffy a wink. He turned back to Naomi. "Bring the ladies into the bar, please." He couldn't take his eyes off the poker she was holding. Could he find blood dried on that iron rod? Would she try to use it on he or Duffy? "Now, Naomi!"

The tone of his voice left no doubt in her mind and she scuttled off down the hallway to find the others and Bull picked up the fireplace poker immediately. His eyes stripped that heavy piece of steel from one end to the other. "Damn," he said, setting it back by the fireplace. "Thought for sure I'd find some of Jake's blood."

"No, Bull," Duffy said. "You hoped you'd find some blood." Bull gave a little humph and walked into the bar where an equally large fire was blazing. He stood with his back to the fire, waiting. "Doc Elroy's a good man, Duffy, I just hope he's also a fine doctor. We can't afford to lose any more suspects. Damndest case I've been on in a long time."

"I just want it to end," Duffy said. "Can't take much more of this cold."

————

SLIM MADE his way around the building and went toward the corrals first. There were two and each had storm stalls in the back. Alongside the corrals was what appeared to be a hay barn and room for a small buggy or wagon, tack, and other items needed for the care of horses and mules. "No animals," he muttered making his way to the first corral.

"If it was one of the working girls who made off with the riding horse and the pack mule, where are those animals?" He looked around for sign of someone leaving but all the fresh snow killed that idea. He was having second thoughts of a third person being one of the girls.

Slim caught himself talking right out, as if Bull and Duffy were still with him. He moved to the hay barn, saw where tack should have been and then caught the least part of a trail left by a team of mules pulling a sleigh. "Leaving, not arriving," Slim muttered and made his way toward the back door. He remembered when the storm had started to ease, when the huge amounts of snow had slowly slowed to just a few flakes falling.

Whoever drove that team out it was just about an hour or so ago. The storm was slowly ending otherwise I'd have never seen that trail that was left. Who was driving that team and what was in the wagon?

He slipped into the kitchen and could hear loud voices in the front of the building and made his way there almost at a run. Bull was loud and mean, saying, "You better have a better answer than that," to a terrified Naomi. A few of the working girls were almost lined up, as for inspection, and Bull was striding back and forth, almost yelling at Naomi.

"I have a worse answer, Bull," Slim said. Bull, Mockingbird, and Duffy were surrounded by the working girls, all as near to the fireplace as they could get. "Someone left here an hour or so ago. About when we noticed the storm calming down. Left with a team of mules and a sleigh."

"Damn," Bull spat it out. "All right, Naomi, tell me again, slowly, what you found. I'm sorry I yelled at you like that, but what you said didn't seem possible. Now, I guess it does." He had a stern yet ironic look on his face. "We came here to find answers, ladies. Big Jake has had the crap beat out of him and might not live." He wasn't surprised at the lack of reaction.

"Little Al had the crap beat out of him and is near death as well. Now, Naomi, tell me again what you found."

She almost collapsed into one of the filthy settees, tears running down her cheeks. "You sent me to bring the girls in, Marshal, and I found them all except for Sweet Maria. She wasn't in her room or the kitchen and when I went into her room, it looked like most of her clothes and personal items were gone." She was almost sobbing by the time she finished and Bull turned to look at Slim and Duffy.

"Well, that answers a whole bunch of our questions," Slim said. "Other than customers, was Sweet Maria known to have a man friend?"

"She talked about Little Al but that was just to get Jake angry. She teased Jake something awful. Worse than any of us." Naomi looked around at the other girls and back at Slim. "That's all I can think of."

"Little Al?" Bull snorted. "Teased Jake? We might need to back up here just a bit, Slim. We think Jake and Little Al were the ones who stole the bank loot from Big Maude, and that maybe Jake then beat on Little Al, but it was Sweet Maria who stole the bank loot from the two men. You with me Slim?"

"All the way big man."

"And now Sweet Maria is on the lam. She might not know that Little Al is out of the picture." Bull looked at Slim who gave a look around the room, getting questions from all the eyes looking back at him.

"If, as we're thinking right now, it was Sweet Maria who drove that team out of here, where might she go? Does she have any friends here in Washoe Valley?" Slim asked. "Is she planning to meet Little Al? Or someone else?" He knew the storm had let up but the roads would be in horrible condition—deep snow, big drifts, possible trees down or creeks running over their banks.

Slim looked at Bull, then Duffy, and back to Naomi. "Where would she go?"

"She always talked about San Francisco," the girl who called herself Angel, said. "She pictured herself as a madam in a whore house near the docks. It was just silly talk."

"Might not be so silly if she had a wagon load of gold and silver," Bull said. "Nevada Territory has two ways out. Over Donner Summit or the Johnson road out of Genoa." He looked at Slim. "Which would you take, Slim?"

"More than likely they would be closed with this storm, but if she knew anything about the area she would opt for Donner. They've done wonders with that road. Making it from here to Lake's Crossing might be tough, making it over Donner would be much more than difficult until crews have had a chance to clear many feet of snow. That's more than eight thousand feet above sea level, Bull."

Bull glared at Angel. "What do you know about all this?"

"I don't know nothing," she wailed. "Just that she always wanted to go to San Francisco. Why would I know anything?" She whimpered and Bull just scowled at her.

Bull looked at the ladies, some sitting now on settees, one near the fire, and one looking out the front windows. Company inspection was over for the time being. "Anybody want to add to this?" He took the time to glower at each person before continuing.

"When Jake and Little Al killed Big Maude, they stole the bank's loot along with all the money that Maude had in the vault back there," and he nodded toward Big Maude's rooms. "Right now, we believe, Sweet Maria might just have all of that tucked away in her wagon. If you know anything, spit it out now."

Slim was thinking the same way as Bull. Did Sweet Maria have help from any of these women? Was there a large conspiracy involving the bunch of them? And, once again, Little Al' name came into play. Was Sweet Maria working with Tyson or Jake?

Bull strode to the fireplace and grabbed the poker, jabbed at the logs burning brightly, and held the poker is both hands, across his body. He took a long look at the poker and then the women. "Well? Where is Maria going? Who is she working with." He slapped that poker into his hand a time or two.

Naomi burst into tears, Angel cringed deeper into the settee, and the girl standing at the window announced, "Company, girls. Company coming." There was a little stir of excitement and then she said, "No, it's just the sheriff. Sheriff Mockingbird ain't a customer."

Mockingbird made his way, painfully, up the snow covered front steps and into the whorehouse parlor. "Glad you're still here," he said. "I'm pretty sure Little Al's dying. I sent the doctor up to the jail and come for you, Bull. If he's gonna tell us anything, you better get over there."

Mockingbird Jessup walked with a limp before meeting up with Bull Morrison and Slim Calhoun but after these last few days of activity at a high level, every bone and muscle in his old body was fighting back. "It sure was easier being a jailer before I met you boys." The two marshals laughed as Slim reached for his heavy coat.

"Let's go, Slim," Bull said. "Duffy, see if you can find out any more about Sweet Maria and her friends." He fought his way into his heavy buffalo robe coat and was out the door, Slim right with him. "Doc ain't gonna appreciate it but we got to talk to that man before he dies."

Many lawmen understand that if a person knows

he's a goner, he just might tell everything he knows and Bull was sure that Little Al knew a lot. Did he know details about the Parker Canyon massacre? About who was behind the killings? Did he kill Maude? Who beat the hell out of Frank Oberlin? Was it Sweet Maria ran off with the loot?

Bull wondered at the same time if maybe he should ask Jake those same questions. *Does Jake know Sweet Maria was sweet on Little Al?* That question might destroy the jail, he chuckled, picturing Jake's reaction. *I'd love to see those two get into it. I'd take on the winner and we'd have some damn answers.*

They didn't wait for Mockingbird, just high stepped it to the jail. Mockingbird could make his own way, what with a gimpy leg and too many years behind him. Did those legs come from too many fights? Or too many young colts needing some training?

Doctor Elroy hadn't arrived yet and they found Little Al in agony, blood pouring from many of the wounds that Doc Elroy had patched up. Tyson was covered in sweat and blood, thrashing against the chains holding him in place. His wrists were bleeding, his ankles were bleeding, and every wound on his head and shoulders were again bleeding.

"He did it to himself," Slim said. "Look, he's ripped the bandages loose, torn at the wounds. He's killing himself, protecting somebody."

"Angel was wrong, Slim," Bull said quietly. "Sweet Maria and Little Al are a couple and he's not going to let us find out what their plan was." Bull remembered his earlier thoughts and looked into Jake's cell.

"You awake, Jake?"

"Who can sleep with that fool screaming all night."

"Looks like Sweet Maria got off with all that money. All that gold that Crazy Ned Paulson stole from the bank. She and Little Al had plans. Did you know that?"

It was quiet in Jake's cell, the one right next to Little Al's. But only for a moment or two. "You ain't gettin' a cent of that, Little Al," Jake screamed through the iron bars separating the cells. "You'll be dead and that foul mouthed whore will spend it all."

Before the conversation could go on, Doctor Elroy came into the cell area. "Now what have you done, Marshal? You people are animals."

"Once again, Doc, you are wrong. He did this to himself. All chained up like that and he was still able to rip those bandages loose. I'm not really sure you should go in there, but I'll be right next to you if you do."

"I have to. That man will be dead in half an hour or less if I don't. He did this to himself? Why?"

"I think he has a lady friend who has all his money and he doesn't want us to know where she is. He's committing suicide, Doc." Bull just shook his head wondering, probably right along with Doc Elroy, why an outlaw as vicious as Tyson, as sadistic as that man is, would protect some woman, a whore, and the money.

"I've been chasing and capturing killers for a long time," Bull said. "Everyone has a strange tale to tell. Tyson here is connected to the recent bank robbery in some way, I'm sure. And the massacre at Parker Canyon, too. He's probably the one who murdered big Maude. You tell me why he would kill himself to protect some working girl who has all that bank loot."

Doctor Elroy just stood there, his little bag of magic medicines in hand, and shook his head slowly back and forth. The sadness in his eyes spoke volumes about the man's humanity. "Ain't no answers to these kinds of questions, Doc," Bull said.

Bull pulled the cell keys from a hook and moved to open the steel door. Little Al was chained to the wall and floor, but his hands could move some, obviously enough to rip bandages loose, and if he tried, he could probably kick enough to hurt someone bad.

Bull handed Slim his big Colt Walker and stepped into the cell. "If you make a move on the doc, Tyson, I'll be forced to knock you senseless so he can make you well." Bull Morrison had an ironic grin on his face. 'That way, we'll be able to hang you." Little Al Tyson growled out something that couldn't be understood, tried to rip the chains from the wall, and slumped forward, only about halfway conscious.

"We was hoping to get some answers from him while you did your patch work, Doc, but it doesn't look like it now. Let's make sure he's almost out." Bull carefully reached out and touched Little Al's eyebrow and the outlaw exploded, trying to grab the marshal, kicking, trying to bite, whipping the chains. Tyson was screaming obscenities and spitting at everyone in the jail.

Bull jumped back and swung one of those saloon destroying right crosses of his, and put the bad man Tyson to sleep. "No answers from you," he said. "Come on in, Doc, it's safe now. I'll be right here."

"I've never seen anything like this in all the years I've been practicing medicine. How did you know he might be pretending?"

"You can look at someone and have an idea what might be wrong with 'em, Doc. Well, all my years of practicing the art of being a U.S. Marshal gives me the knowledge that there are people who simply can't do the right thing. Tyson is one of them. Might call it just a hunch that he was playing possum."

"I'm gonna get back to Big Maude's," Slim said. "Gotta assume that our get-away girl is our third person, and we gotta get on the trail if a trail even exists. Mockingbird will get here eventually and you can catch up."

Bull grimaced, said some nasty words under his breath and helped the doctor get his stuff arranged. "Make sure I know where you're going if you and Duffy take off," Bull growled and Slim chuckled walking out of the jail.

"You bet, Marshal."

CHAPTER 24

THE ROAD WAS IN TERRIBLE CONDITION AS SWEET MARIA drove the mules south out of Washoe City and along the east shore of Washoe Lake. Drifts were incredibly deep, trees were downed all along the way, rock and snow slides made travel more than difficult and dangerous. Normally, the drive from Washoe City to Nevada Territory's Capitol of Carson City would be just a few hours, but in these conditions, Sweet Maria didn't have any idea. All she knew was she had to keep going, had to be in Carson City before dark. Little Al would be waiting for her at the livery stables.

The mules were in good condition for this time of the year, but Sweet Maria had to stop often and let them blow. Plowing through deep snow pulling a heavy wagon was taking a toll on the animals. From time to time they had to get off the road and make their way around downed trees and the fear of falling into a drainage ditch was foremost in Sweet Maria's mind.

Making that kind of ride in those conditions after sunset would be an open invitation to death and Sweet

Maria knew it. She had to be in Carson City before dark or find someplace to hide for the night. Was Little Al there? Did he kill Jake and make his escape? All she knew was, Little Al told her to make her run to the capitol as soon as the storm broke.

Make my way to Carson City, she almost laughed at the thought. *It was all I could do to make my way from the Lakeside Inn to the Pleasure Palace.* She shook her head watching the mules fight their way forward. "Ain't gonna make Carson City today, tonight, or maybe even tomorrow." She spat the words out, and eased her anger back some.

"Ain't your fault, boys," she said, and talked gentle to them, urging them on. She would have to stop again, soon, to let them catch their breath. "I'm gonna spend tonight under this wagon just sure as hell," she chuckled.

It was such an easy plan and Maria's part was the most dangerous in her mind. The fact that Little Al had to kill Jake when they met up at the Lakeside Inn wasn't that hard in her mind. She did not know what the rest of the plan was. Just meet Little Al and he would tell her then. She had a little pocket pistol in her rabbit skin muff, .32 caliber with two shots, in case she was stopped.

Both the mules had been under harness many times and were known to be well trained and have decent personalities. Sweet Maria, straight off a family farm in Missouri, had been driving mules since she was old enough to climb onto a wagon. She could pick out where the road was by the bushes and trees alongside, and the animals were in good shape.

It was the cold that bothered the girl. "Wind's coming right off the lake, mules," She whispered through her muffler. She even had a scarf wrapped around the fake fur muffler, but her nose was running and her ears were frozen. "Ain't gonna make Carson City," she moaned. It was easy, on a long drive like this, to let her mind wander and for the first time in a long while her mind was on a farm way back in Missouri. "That was a long time ago."

These thoughts may have been brought on by having reins in hand sitting behind two well trained mules. It may have been brought on by feeling free for the first time in many years. She wasn't under the thumb of some mean gambling man, wasn't being ordered around by Big Maude or mauled by Jake. She stiffened up at the thought.

"I am free. I have a wagon filled with thousands of dollars and nobody telling me what to do." The thought raged through her mind as she continued south through deep drifts, strong winds blowing snow but clouds slowing moving out of the picture. *Little Al said if I messed up he would chase me down and kill me. He ain't got a good thought for another person at all. Why am I thinking about running off with that fool? Why did I run off with that gambling man? Why can't I just do something right? Something just for me?*

While those thoughts were important, Sweet Maria quickly caught up the mules when they began to veer off the main road. Wind had played havoc with the landscape. There were few dips, culverts, or holes visible. Everything was flat so walking the mules into a culvert was possible. The trees along the roadway, mostly cottonwood along with some pine had taken the brunt of the storm and branches had been ripped free, whole trees toppled, and in places, closed the road.

Broken cottonwood trees slowed Sweet Maria, sometimes almost to a halt. She forced the mules to thrash through deep drifts, working their way around the broken and downed trees, and she had to stop often to let the beasts catch their breath. It was frigid and she knew for certain she would not make it to Cason City before night fell. Being out on the road after night fell would mean death. She was not prepared for that. There were no blankets, no food, no medical supplies in the wagon.

Stupid. I'm being stupid again. Wake up, Maria. Wake up, damn it. Papa told me how many times, 'You got a blanket with you?' Well, Papa, I don't and you were always right. Don't go workin' in the fields without something to protect you from storms that pop up from nowhere. This ain't a Missouri storm, Papa, but it's sure achin' to kill me.

She'd heard stories as a child back in Missouri about travelers dying from the cold, their frozen bodies being found in all types of contortionist poses. Some said it's just a case of going to sleep, others spoke of incredible torture as the body froze. She was too young to ask, "How would you know, you've never frozen to death?" She couldn't keep all the old stories quiet. She couldn't keep her papa quiet. She was still berating herself even as the other's did.

Visibility was excellent with the storm's exit, a few lingering bright white clouds scudding slowly across the high ridges of the Sierra Nevada, the snow on the ground so damned bright forced her to wrap her scarf over her eyes. It hampered her vision some but she also didn't go snow blind. She was able to see through the knitted thread but did worry about the mules.

This is taking too long. I ain't never gonna get to Carson

City today. I gotta find a place, a ranch or even a deadfall off the road. Sweet Maria had some frontier skills, like making a fire, making a camp out of the wind, having her bedroll close to the fire. It was that thought that almost brought panic to Sweet Maria's world.

Bedroll. I ain't got no bedroll. She started thinking of everything she brought down to the wagon. Her clothes, yes, boots and shoes, her little gun, and, of course, all those bags of money. No bedroll. *No blankets, but I do have all those winter coats and all those dresses. I can make up a bedroll.*

She was trying to think of what she would need to make up a camp for one night. *Only gonna be there overnight. I can make up a bedroll. Fire. I'm gonna need a good fire. I have my knife, my flint, but I ain't got no ax. Where am I gonna find dry wood?* The weight of sheer panic was heavy and it wasn't long before tears were freezing to her cheeks.

One of the old Missouri tales dealt with madness during the slow freezing of a traveler in winter. Often, she remembered, the victim went mad, crazy, nuts, and did all the wrong things, all the things that were sure to lead to a terrible and painful death.

She was thirteen when she ran away from the family farm, tied up with a fast talking gambling man, and made her way toward the goldfields of California. She left him somewhere in Nebraska country, partnered up with another sly fellow, and he left her off in Washoe City. She knew about camping, she knew about death on the emigrant trail, and she knew she was in desperate trouble.

I ain't gonna panic, ain't gonna cry, ain't gonna die. I ain't. She had been on the road to Carson City a few times, knew the road circled around the south end of Washoe Lake and then climbed over Lakeview Hill before dropping into Eagle Valley and into Carson City. With the storm gone and visibility good, she knew she was close to the south end of the lake but still a long way to go with just a short amount of time before nightfall.

The road made a turn around a steep shoulder of the mountains that dipped almost to the lake's edge. She had to drive the mules almost into the water to get around the rocks, and then the road climbed up and around more large rocks. As she brought the mules back down she spotted a building off to her right. It sat on a hillock surrounded by cottonwood trees and the roadway seemed to run right up to it.

There was no smoke from the chimney as she pulled the mules up to a hitching rack. She fumbled inside her muff, pulled her pistol out, and struggled to climb down from the wagon. She had been sitting for hours, almost frozen in place, was so stiff and cold she almost fell on her face. It took a few moments to get her balance, found she could walk but stiffly, and made her way through the deep snow to the cabin door.

There was no answer when she pounded and she tried the latch, almost yelling out when the door opened. "My god almighty don't shoot," she screamed, but there was no one there and she slipped inside. "It's a saloon," she almost whispered. She found a lantern and got it lit, found others and got them lit, and found a bottle of whiskey and took a long drink. "I ain't gonna die," she said right out. "I ain't."

There was a fireplace, stacked wood and kindling, and Sweet Maria had a smile as she put together a fire.

Wadded up paper, some dry grass, a sprinkle of whiskey and a strike on the flint. She slowly added larger and larger pieces of wood to the hot flames and had a scorcher going in minutes. "I'll sleep warm and be on my way to Carson City at first light." Food never entered the girl's mind.

The night was filled with ugly scenes of people freezing to death, of mules standing guard over a dead little girl, of her father asking if she had a blanket. But Sweet Maria was warm. She awakened twice to stoke the fire, and deep sleep came after the second awakening.

———

"WHAT DO WE KNOW, DUFFY?" Slim moved quickly to the fire to shuck off his heavy coat. "Doc and Bull are with Little Al. Ain't gonna learn nothing from that fool."

"I sent the girls off. Crying women don't make it with me. There's coffee in the kitchen, though. Took a walk around back, where you were, and it looks like whoever drove that sleigh went south. All mingled with other tracks once the sleigh moved onto one of the streets, though."

"Bull is sure that Sweet Maria is our third person and is sure that she was attached to Little Al. He had that pigsty of a saloon at the south end of the lake. Suppose she's trying to make that run? Difficult at best."

"Not fun on a good day but she has purpose, Slim. It's often called gold."

Slim laughed right out as he made his way to the kitchen and hot coffee. "I don't think we have to be in any kind of hurry. It's going to be dark in just a few hours and we sure don't want to be caught on that trail after dark. Oh, no."

"Tyson must have had a plan of some kind, Slim. She must think he's waiting for her at his place and they would leave out, maybe in the morning. Or he would. He prefers being a loner. She's bringing him all the money, but she might not be in the plans to run off. She won't know that he's sitting in jail about half dead."

"She don't, Duffy. Expect we'll find her body and a couple of mules standing guard over thousands of dollars. We'll leave at first light. Let's ride light, just some smoked meat and coffee beans in the saddle bags, our bedrolls, and plenty of ammunition."

"Blankets, Slim. Bedrolls and extra blankets. Just in case."

The marshals made their way to the jail to bring Bull Morrison up to date. The doc wasn't able to save Tyson. "Damn fool was smiling when the last of his poisoned blood fell to the floor, still fighting his chains. He took a lot of our answers with him, I'm afraid."

"Did you get a chance to talk to Jake?"

"He's hurtin' bad but ain't gonna die. Got some busted up ribs, bad cuts all over his body, and bruises. Wasn't willing to talk and I figured we'd let him heal up some before we get serious about answers. He's got 'em, I'm sure. We just got to ask the right questions."

Bull led them back to Uncle Bob's Café for a much needed supper. "All three of us will ride at first light."

"Shame you didn't get anything more from Jake. It must have come as a surprise to him to find out Sweet Maria was running with Little Al." Slim had to chuckle remembering Jake's response.

"Man never said another word," Bull said. "I couldn't

do much prodding, either, what with all the commotion caused by Tyson. As I said, we'll wait."

It was busy in the café, half the town out walking through the snow but enjoying blue skies and bright sunshine late in the afternoon. The table by the window was available and they fought their way out of heavy winter coats and took their seats. Celinda O'Mally was at Slim's side in seconds.

"About time you showed up, big boy. Hello, Bull, Mike. You can't keep this fine young marshal away from me like that. He needs his nourishing and..." She smiled down at Slim's eager face. "Want something hot?"

Slim gulped, tried to say something, but Celinda cut him off.

"To eat?"

Bull Morrison was roaring, slapped the table, and pointed at Slim. "You're red as the ace of hearts," he almost yelled out at the crowd, now all going out of their way to look at Slim. Celinda didn't lose a beat. She bent down and kissed Slim right on the mouth, stood up straight, took a deep breath, and slowly sank into his lap.

The café exploded with laughter, thunderous applause, all led by Bull Morrison. "I ain't never seen nothing like that in all my life," Mike Duffy laughed. "You been had, boy," he almost yelled. "You're hooked and there ain't nothing you can do about it."

It took until supper was half eaten for the crimson to leave Slim's neck and cheeks, but the comments never let up. "We got to take the time to talk about tomorrow," he said. His eyes were narrowed, his mouth set grim like, and his fists tight, sitting on the edge of the supper table.

"What's tomorrow?" Duffy asked. "Wedding day?" He said it loud enough for those at close tables could hear and the laughter and hoots started all over again.

"We'll talk on the walk back to the hotel," Bull said. He was still laughing getting up and finding his coat. "Gonna be a long walk back. I think."

Celinda stood near the front desk and Slim walked up to pay the bill. "I hope you've had your fun," he almost snarled.

"Oh, Slim, I ain't even started." She threw herself at him, wrapped her arms around his neck and kissed him again, only this time it was a long, slow, very deliberate kiss that had tons of meaning behind it. "Ain't even begun," she smiled, backing away. "You catch all your outlaws, put everybody in jail that you have to, and then it will be time for you and me. Don't be late, Slim Calhoun."

His knees almost buckled, his eyes were swimming in pools of lust, and he allowed her to gently shove him toward the door, held open by Mike Duffy. Those words *don't be late* would echo in his head for a long time.

CHAPTER 25

WASHOE VALLEY DIDN'T SEE THE SUN UNTIL SEVERAL hours after first light, buried as it is between the Virginia Range on the east and the Sierra Nevada on the west. "It's gotta be a long way below zero," Duffy said, pulling his cinch tight. "At least there's no wind."

"Hasn't been any, either," Slim said. "Gonna make for a cold ride but if we find tracks from a couple of mules and a gold laden wagon, we'll keep warm."

Slim Calhoun had chased bad men with Bull Morrison for several years, but this current effort seemed so strange, so much difference from what might be called a run-of-the-mill bank robbery. And, how did a runaway prostitute fit into the package? "We ain't never worked anything like this, Bull. The loot is all from a single robbery yet we've got half a dozen different crimes we're working on."

Bull laughed thinking about it. "Crazy Ned Paulson couldn't conceive of anything this crazy if he worked on it. That twenty thousand dollars has been in the hands of half a dozen thieves and most of 'em are dead.

Little Sweet Maria doesn't know how much trouble she's in."

Slim nodded, thinking about that. Was she working with Jake? Or was she running away with the loot to be with Little Al? *There's a third part of this I've tried my best to not think about. Is Sweet Maria not running away to be with either of those men but rather to be alone in the world with twenty thousand dollars?* He chuckled as the thought made its way deeper. *She just might be a whole lot smarter than we think.*

The mule and wagon tracks were more than evident as the three marshals left the town and moved along the road to Carson City. Winds had whipped things up but they weren't sustained winds and the tracks the mules left were easy to follow.

"Ain't no one been along here since our little dove," Duffy said. The cottonwood trees' limbs hung as if in sorrow, carrying massive burdens of ice and snow. Many simply gave up, broke off, and made the trail that much more difficult. They followed the tracks that Sweet Maria left them as she made her way around broken trees.

"Either she knows how to drive a team or she's got some help," Slim said.

"If she's got help it don't matter much to me. Just one more body to bring back to town," Bull snarled.

"How far is it to Little Al's joint, Bull? You've been there." Slim had his shawl wrapped around his face to keep from going snow blind, while at the same time trying to take in all the beauty of an early morning along the shore of Washoe Lake and the majestic Sierra Nevada. The wind had sculpted magnificent works of art from the offered landscape, trees bent in submission to the proffered loads of snow, and the trail remained more than obvious.

"Less than ten miles," Bull said. "Little Al was planning to kill off Jake when they got to the Lakeside Inn, and Jake was planning to kill off Little Al. I'm wondering if Sweet Maria knows what the outcome was? Her job was to grab the loot and carry it off to meet later with Little Al."

"That's almost funny when you stop to think about it." Slim said. "Sweet Maria doesn't know that Little Al ain't gonna meet up with her. Doesn't know he got the tar beat out of him and is dead."

"I don't think we ever mentioned any of that when she was around," Duffy said. "I did find out how Jake got beat up. It was the girls led by Sweet Maria and Angel. I wonder if something was said?"

"I'm still wondering if Sweet Maria might be working for herself," Slim said. The comment caught the two other marshals by surprise and got both of them thinking.

"Don't matter none," Bull said. "We'll find her, return the bank's money, and get the hell out of Nevada Territory. I could eat a bear right now. I'm cold and don't like that either. Might just shoot her whether she gives up or not."

"Glad you're feeling better," Slim quipped.

————

THERE WERE STILL coals in the fireplace when Maria woke up. She had wrapped herself in layers of her clothing and was laid out on the plank floor in front of the fireplace. "Sunrise? I just got here," she moaned, trying to get herself unwrapped from the mess she had made. She stirred the coals, added kindling, and with a little blowing, had a goodly fire going in minutes. It brought back memories of her younger days on the farm back in Missouri.

Pa always said getting the morning fires going was up to me and Ma. Said he didn't have time for such nonsense, that he could get along just fine in the cold. I think he was funnin' us but I'm still not really sure. Pa always said my fires were the warmest. Stupid girl, runnin' away like I did.

She realized that those thoughts had danced around in her dreams all night long. *I ain't gonna be a stupid little girl no more. Done with being stupid. From now on, Maria, my pet, you will be a thinking girl, and one with a bit of money to help.*

The old building wasn't built to hold warm air inside but the heat from the fireplace did an adequate job keeping things warm. She could still see her breath, but bundled up and standing near the fire she was all right. "Gotta be some coffee around here someplace," she muttered. She was behind the single plank bar moving bottles around and found the grinder, eventually finding some beans in a bowl.

The coffee boiled quickly and with some added whiskey, Sweet Maria was ready for a new day. "Gotta get to Carson City and it ain't that far." She found a stash of smoked venison and chewed on it as she put her things back together. She felt bad about leaving the mules harnessed all night, but it was so cold she didn't think she would be able to get them harnessed in the morning. She had spread some hay she found for them and walked them down to the lake where they pawed at the shoreline ice and got something to drink.

"Just a few hours from now I'll feel those huge arms around me and I'll be warm as fresh apple pie." *Pa used to say that, and he'd reach over and pinch Ma's butt. Ain't thought about that for a long time.* The mules were slow getting into a good rhythm but Maria let them find it on their own. They blew enough steam to almost look like an engine with legs, she thought, moving toward Lakeview Hill. It was a cold morning but she thrilled at the bright sun.

Sun finally peaked over the Virginia Range and blasted down into Washoe Valley. The sight took her breath away. Every mountain, hillside, tree, rock, and meadow was sculpted in snow and ice, the iced over lake, with no wind, shown as a giant mirror. Flocks of Canadian Geese were flying out from their lakeside nests for fields of grass nearby, while great flights of spoonbills, mallards, and grayback ducks made their way to the waters below.

The mules knew how to stay on the pathway and Maria couldn't take her eyes off the beauty of Washoe Valley. Those high peaks of Slide Mountain and Mount Rose towered above the valley and she could see morning winds at those high altitudes blowing snow off the ridge crests giving the idea of a crown of jewels in the bright sun.

"Ain't nothing like this in Missouri," she chuckled. She had some jerky to chew on, did remember to bring a flask of water but it was probably just a block of ice now. She rounded the southern shore of Washoe Lake and turned south to begin the climb over Lakeview Hill. It wasn't long and she noticed the mules having more and more difficulty.

"Heavy load," she murmured. She got the whip out,

not to beat the animals but to urge them on. Just a flick or two to keep their minds on their job. The snow was deep and the mules had a long hard trip the day before, didn't have the pleasure of a good night, and were asked to pull a wagon loaded with gold over a high ridge. Maria's wagon was the first on the road since the storm. "Come on, boys," she hollered, flicking them with the whip. "Just a little more and we'll top this old hill off," she yelled.

Thoughts of Missouri crowded in, and they were good thoughts. She remembered a stupid argument with her pa, remembered running off with that no-good gambler. "Dumb," she said. "I ain't cut out to be a whore. This is where I belong, behind a couple of mules, pulling a plow or a wagon load of wheat or corn. Shouldn't a done what I did."

There was a smile on her face, a real one, not something forced toward a mill worker with two dollars stuck in his filthy hands. Her eyes sparkled in the morning light and she never even gave her load a thought. Twenty thousand dollars sitting under canvas wrap in the back of that wagon and Maria never gave it a thought. "Ain't never been this free in my life."

Now she was tied up with a man far more dangerous than a two-bit gambling man, a man who took great pleasure in hurting people. She couldn't help remembering what they said about Big Maude when her body was found and knew that Little Al Tyson was responsible. It had been fun, though, those nights when he carried her off into the forest. They were rough affairs and he'd bring her back to the Pleasure Palace with cuts and bruises. "Ain't gonna be doing dumb things anymore. Stupid," she snarled at the mules. "Let's go, boys. Come on, just a little bit more and we'll be over the crest."

The mules were tired to the bone, but the flicks to their back sides kept them moving, one plodding foot in front of the other. Maria kept up her calling out, just as she had done as a young girl running a plow or a wagon back on the farm. Her Pa taught her how to run a straight line, but there was more than one trip behind the barn before she learned to listen good.

God how I'd love to be back there right now. How did I get into this? No, dumb girl, how do I get out of this? Her mind was active, wouldn't let go. *Cain't go home. Ain't got no home other than Big Maude's. Ma and Pa wouldn't let me in, anyways. Cain't stay with Little Al. He'll get tired of me and just throw me out or kill me. Damn stupid girl.*

Eagle Valley spread out below as she topped off Lakeview Hill. She could see where the Carson River was, far off to the southeast, could see the small village of the Nevada Territorial Capitol, and wondered how long she still had to go and whether Little Al would be there to meet her. *I'll leave off this wagon and run away,* she mused and then sat bolt upright in the wagon seat. *Hell I will. I'll grab a pocket full of that gold and then I'll leave out.* She was almost laughing as she led the mules down the hillside to Carson City. The team was breathing easier, and so was Sweet Maria.

Maria was still an attractive woman, still young in years but well-aged in life. She wore too much rouge, too much stinking perfume, and dressed as a trollop, but she could still remember wearing her older brother's overalls, tugging on heavy oversized boots, trying to climb into the big wagon while her pa held the team. *Me and a pocket full of gold coins are going to leave out of Nevada Territory on the first stage east.*

———

"It ain't much to look at, is it?" Slim said as the three marshals rode up to the front of Little Al's saloon. There were no animals in the corrals but it was obvious that a team of mules hauled a sleigh out just a few hours ago. "Let's check out inside quick, boys and get back on the trail. She can't be too far ahead of us."

"No," Bull said. "She got out of here about the same time we left Washoe City. Let's ride, boys. She gets into Carson City we'll have a hell of a time finding her. We don't know if she planned to meet Little Al at some specific place or what. We don't know if she has friends there as well. Let's ride." He was right and Slim knew it.

Bull pulled his horse around and laid the spurs to him and the others followed at a comfortable lope through snow about two feet deep. Bull pulled back quickly and let his horse set the gate. "Ain't no reason to take it out on the horses," he mumbled. They came to the split in the trail, one continuing west toward Franktown and the other bending south toward Lakeview Hill and they followed the mules' tracks.

"That wagon is heavy," Slim said. "And those mules are tired. She ran them animals hard yesterday and they ain't pleased with this morning. The bank said it lost around twenty thousand dollars, mostly in gold coins. That's a heavy load for two mules going up an icy and steep hill."

Even for those horseback, the climb up Lakeview Hill from the north was hard on the animals. They crested out and Bull called for a quick rest stop. "Looks like our little girl with the gold took a rest here as well," he said. The small village of Carson City sparkled in the bright sun, it's square set streets and pathways took up a very small space in the overall panorama. Streets were lined with trees, mostly cottonwood and elm, and here and there, a fruit tree. "She's still got a good lead on us, boys. Ain't gonna kill the animals but we can't let that gold get away from us."

CHAPTER 26

"Don't see something like that very often," Silas Thornberry said, sweeping dirt and debris from the wooden walkway in front of his dry-goods emporium. "She ain't exactly dressed to be a damn muleskinner, eh?" The two men standing with old Silas laughed right out. Snow had been shoveled off the walkway but men and women moving about carried mud everywhere. "You just come in from Strawberry?" he yelled out to Maria.

"Washoe City," she yelled back. "Know where Roop Street is? Got a delivery," she lied.

Thornberry looked at the wagon and it definitely was loaded with something, but Maria didn't fit in the picture. She was wearing a dress, not heavy canvas pants. She had two or three women's jackets on, not a buffalo robe or bear skin coat. *That gal's got spunk dressed like that in this weather. Or just too dumb to dress properly.*

"Take a left at the intersection and go two blocks. Ain't much down that way," he hollered. "What'cha carrying? Looks heavy."

"Ice," she yelled back. *What made me say that? Damn, now somebody's sure to get all involved. Shoulda just rode right on by.* "New business my Pa wants to get started. Next load, it'll be four mules, not two." She gave the team a little flick to keep them moving.

She came to the intersection, found a considerable number of people out and about, many seemingly looking right at her. *Gotta find Jenkins Livery and Freight Company. Little Al said they would be expecting me and to wait there for him.* It had snowed in Carson City but not as much as in Washoe Valley and at times the sleigh's runners were in the mud as much as snow and ice. The mules were tired but pulled them though the mess.

She made the turn onto Roop Street and saw the livery sign and several horses at a rack out front. She pulled up to the big gates that led into the corrals, a barn, blacksmith shop, and a large building where buggies and wagons were being built.

"Wonder how Little Al knew about this place?" she murmured, watching someone approach. A skinny old man, bald as the day he was born but wearing a massive beard, some white, some black, some tobacco stained, limped out of the barn. He had bright green eyes and she imagined she saw a smile under his huge beard. His large hands stood out some and the fingers and knuckles were well gnarled. She saw a lot of hard work in those hands.

"Looking for Al Tyson," she called out.

"Ain't seen that foul mouthed bastard in weeks." He spat out some tobacco juice, gave Maria a sideways look, and didn't apologize for his remarks either. "What makes you think he'd be here?" The words had an angry cast to them but weren't said in anger.

She smiled, thinking back to her young times on the farm. *Pa talked like that. Tried to make you think he was all angry and upset. Kept me on my toes. I bet this old man takes good care of his wife.*

"Said to meet him here," she said. "Where can a girl get something good to eat?" She was weak with cold and hunger, and had a plan all worked out. *For the first time in a long time I know where I'm goin' and how to get there.* She paid almost no attention to the mules during the last five miles or so coming into town, working this plan through her head.

"Park that mess over there. Mules can go in the second corral, there's feed and water. Be half a dollar for each of the mules a day, and another half a dollar to park the wagon. In advance, girl."

"That's what Tyson said." She moved the wagon to where he had pointed and climbed down. Her hands were so cold she had a hard time working them and the old man jumped in to help.

"What's a little woman like you doing running a team like this?" He had the team undressed in nothing flat. "Name's Jenkins. What's a nice woman like you doing even knowing Tyson?"

"This is his wagon. I've got some stuff I need to get and you can tell me where to get something to eat. If he ain't here yet, he'll be here soon." *He's about half right,* she thought. *What am I doing here? I've embarrassed myself, selling my body, ruined my reputation, and now, being associated with the likes of Little Al. Well, Mr. Jenkins, this time tomorrow I'm gonna be a long way from here and won't nobody know I've been a whore.*

Maria clambered her way into the back of the wagon, doing her best not to answer his questions. She opened one of the heavy feed sacks and took in a big breath of cold air. "Oh my God," she muttered. She looked around quickly, made sure no one could see what she saw.

Sweet Maria was fully aware that she was packing the loot from the bank robbery but it never occurred to her what exactly twenty thousand dollars in gold coins might look like. Mostly twenty-dollar double eagles, they glittered and shone, piercingly bright. She reached in and grabbed a handful and shoved them in her jacket pocket and started to close the sack.

"Ain't gonna be stupid about this," she muttered and grabbed a second handful. She had picked up six or seven coins with each grab and had one handful in a left pocket and the other on the right. "No wonder those mules ain't happy," she chuckled as she climbed down off the wagon.

"I'll just leave everything else until Little Al gets here," she said. She smiled a bright sunshiny smile at Jenkins, straightened her skirts, and asked again where she could get something to eat.

"Best bet would be the Silver Dollar Café," he said. He pointed up Telegraph Street. "It's right in town, near that new capitol building. got a sign out front. Looks like you owe me about three dollars, Miss."

"I calculate two-fifty Mr. Jenkins, but if you give those old mules an extra helping of oats I'll make it three. I'll need change. Little Al only gave me a single coin. He can be tight, you know." She had never felt as free as she did that moment, handing Jenkins a double eagle.

"Oh, I forgot something," she said and climbed back into the wagon. She rustled through her stuff and found a shoulder strap carpet bag, opened a feed sack, and shoved fifteen or more coins in it. Grabbed a few more, closed the sack, and climbed down.

"Now I got everything. Thank you." She smiled at Jenkins, turned and walked out of the stables. The Silver Dollar Café was reasonably busy this late in the day and she found a table, ordered the early supper special and coffee.

"Where is the stage office? I just don't know my way around at all," she said.

"About half a block north of where we are," the waiter said. "Which way you going?

"East," she said. "Missouri, eventually."

"The east bound will be leaving in an hour or so, I think. That's a long ride in one of those horrible mail wagons." He was about twenty, first job for the boy, and Sweet Maria was an attractive young woman. "I think there's an evening coach out in about an hour."

The warm food, several cups of hot coffee, and Maria was ready to make her way to the stage office. *Last time I felt this way is when I made the biggest mistake of my life. What I'm about to do ain't no mistake.* Memories of when she ran off with the gambling man were being set aside by thoughts of climbing in that stage with tickets giving her a ride home.

Ain't never heard a word from Ma or Pa in the years I've been gone. Are they even alive? Ma was always sickly, never did eat right, and Pa worked too hard at that rock pit he called a farm. She felt the warm trickle of a tear making its way down her cheek, wiped it away, tried to replace it with a scowl, and got to her feet.

Damn carpet bag is heavy, she almost muttered. She looked around quickly and made her way out of the café and onto the busy main street of Nevada Territory's capitol city. The stage office wasn't crowded and the clerk was a grumpy older man who didn't even look up when she approached.

"Ain't sure how to go about this," she said. "Need to buy a ticket to Missouri."

"That's a long ride, Miss. Gonna cost you about fifty bucks or more plus you gotta buy your own food at the food stops. You'll ride the coach from here to Salt Lake City, then change to another one for the rest of the trip. You'll be a mess when you get there."

"Don't have to go to Lake's Crossing?"

"Hell no. Why'd you want to go there? No, the main road is right out east from here." The emigrant trail is how he described it. He put together a sheaf of papers for her, collected money, and looked down at her feet. "Where are your bags?"

"Going as I am," she said. "What I need is right here in my carpet bag. Going home."

"Don't know where your home is but the stage will take you to St. Louis. Be leaving in about half an hour. Make yourself comfortable near the fire." He reached out behind him and came up with a red point blanket, eased from his chair and walked to the door.

"Here, Missy. I think you'll need this. Nice old lady left it a time back. You take it."

People being nice, she thought. Wouldn't be if they knew I was a whore. *Well dammit, I ain't one.* "Thank you. That's very nice."

CHAPTER 27

BULL WAS IN THE LEAD WITH SLIM AND DUFFY LINED OUT behind as they made their way down off Lakeview Hill. The day was getting long, the horses were tired, and Bull knew they would find his starved body alongside the road sometime in the future. "We ain't had nothing to eat but cold hard venison jerky for hours, boys. I gotta get something in my belly soon."

Slim rode up alongside and smiled at his boss. "You thinking buffalo steaks or are you thinking John Barleycorn?"

"Either one right now or both would be better. We get into town, we'll make a quick ride around, see if we can spot that wagon but we gotta eat soon. How many stables are there right in town?"

"The one we've used before is Jenkins' place. Just a block or two from the St. Charles Hotel, if you remember. Might be others. Don't know for sure."

Small talk about bank robbers, murderers, and thieves interspersed with comments about whores running off with twenty thousand dollars in gold coins took up the hour or so it took to ride into town. They were able to see where Maria and the mules made a turn off the main road, and then another turn onto Roop Street. Sleigh runners in the mud stood out some.

"Hell, boys, we might just ride right up onto that wagon." Before turning off the main road east, the Emigrant Trail, they watched a stage head out of town, six horses at a good lope, blowing steam out their nostrils and flinging mud everywhere. "Highballing it to Salt Lake City, she is. Those drivers love to show off their ponies, don't they?"

"Stuffed in the back, having to share space with heavy canvas mail bags, other passengers, and fighting the cold. I'd prefer walking to that ride," Duffy said. "There's Jenkins Stables just ahead, Bull. I've been froze to this saddle since leaving Washoe City. Don't know if I can even get down."

The three marshals rode up to the stable's gates and all three proved just how stiff they were stepping down. "Still better than walking," Bull said. He walked into the big yard and saw Jenkins standing near a hot forge. "Seen a young woman driving a team of mules, old man?"

"Don't answer to old man, mister. Name's Jenkins. Who wants to know?"

Bull Morrison chuckled at the response and pulled his heavy coat aside letting the old man see his badge. "I do. U.S. Marshal Bull Morrison, Mr. Jenkins," he said with a deep bow and broad smile. "I'll bet you were a pip in your day." He looked around to Slim and Duffy. "Now, about a young woman driving a team of mules."

"The mules are right there," he said, pointing at them, "and the wagon's right there. She's over at the café gettin' warm. Said the wagon belongs to that fool Little Al Tyson and that he'd be here to pick it up."

"She just walked off?" Slim asked. "What'd she take with her?"

"All she had was a shoulder strap carpet bag. Looked heavy, but she said that was all she needed." Jenkins ran his fingers through his flowing beard. "You boys seem mighty interested in something."

"Well, you might say that," Bull said. "The wagon don't belong to Little Al. Fact is, Little Al is dead so he won't be coming to see you." Bull turned to Slim. "Ain't no way she's hauled them sacks off. Why don't you climb up there and check?" Then he turned back to Jenkins.

'Where's that café you said she'd be at?"

Slim gave out with a loud whooie and held up one of the feed sacks. "Hit the bonanza we did, Bull. Bet that carpet bag of Sweet Maria's is full of some of these cartwheels, but most all of the bank loot is right here. That feisty old bank manager is gonna be happy to see this mess."

"Duffy, stay here with the loot and mules. Slim, let's go find Sweet Maria. She needs a good talking to." He chuckled as he turned to Jenkins. "We'll be taking the wagon and mules back to Washoe City in the morning, Mr. Jenkins. You can plan on the three of us sleeping in your barn tonight."

"Be fifty cents each, Marshal. Another fifty cents if you want to be grained, too." He tried his best to hold in the cackle but finally let it explode. Slim and Duffy, too, to Bull's chagrin.

———

"WELL, if that don't just beat all hell," Slim said. He and Bull were standing at the ticket window in the stage office shaking their heads. "You sure she said Missouri?"

"Oh, my yes," the clerk said. "She was a pretty girl. Said she was going home. I sold her tickets to St. Louis. Paid me with double eagles, she did. She climbed in that carriage and settled down on a mail sack, using her carpet bag for a pillow and had the prettiest smile on her face."

"I bet she did," Bull said. "Bless her sweet heart, Slim. Let's go. We got us some ridin' to do. That stage will stop at Dayton, Buckland Station, and again near Ragtown. We're well behind so we can ride on through Dayton and probably connect at Buckland Station. Road follows the Carson River the whole way and it's a good one."

"I ain't sure we should even do this. She can't possibly have any more than a hundred or two, it's sunset, and we ain't had a bite to eat in more than five days that I can think of."

Bull laughed, eased back in the saddle and looked at Slim, contemplating what the man said. "Let's just ride out at a nice trot, and I'll tell you why I want to catch that girl. You might still talk me out of continuing, but let's at least start."

"All right, Bull, but remember, we have the loot, we have the only two men who survived this entire fiasco, even though one of them is now dead, so you're gonna have to have a good argument to convince me."

They picked up the Emigrant Trail Road east and rode into what was already twilight. The air had more than a chill to it and the men were wrapped tight in heavy buffalo robes riding at a miles eating trot, chasing a stage driven by six-up, hours ahead of them.

"I didn't think much of Sweet Maria when we talked with the ladies at Big Maude's," Bull said. "She wasn't a hard case like most whores are. Didn't come off as someone who might slip you a knock-out punch or even a shiv, and rip every penny from your pocket or poke."

"Exactly how do you mean?" Slim asked.

"She didn't have her heart in what she was doing. She's a farm girl, Slim. She ain't a down-and-out loser."

"Ain't so sure of that," Slim said. "After all, she was tied up in some way with Little Al Tyson. Don't think your average farm girl would be attracted to him, Jake? Maybe. Not Tyson."

"If she thought she could get her hands on some of that money from the bank robbery, she might be," Bull said. "Here's what I think, Slim. I think there was a lot of talk among the girls after that bank robbery and the massacre at Parker Canyon, and part of that talk had to do with the money being missing."

"I see where you're going. Maude turns up dead, Jake goes missing, and Little Al is suggesting he is going to get his hands on the money."

"You got it, partner. That's when Sweet Maria starts her own little set of plans. She ain't a crook, Slim, even though she did run off with twenty thousand dollars." He and Slim both laughed right out. "But, she only took enough to run away from the life of a whore in Nevada Territory."

"You just blew your own argument on why we should chase her down." Slim said. "She isn't the crook, the killer outlaw. Jake and Tyson are our real targets.

We're chasing a little lost girl trying her best to get back home."

Bull slowly brought his horse to a stop and looked at Slim. They were approaching the Carson River canyon east of town, the sunshine was gone, the night sky was filled with an amazing display of light, and the canyon wind was bitter cold. "Talked myself right out of a nice long, cold, chase through the Nevada deserts, I did. Good job, Bull Morrison. Good job," Bull said.

They turned the horses and rode back toward the capitol city at a casual walk, enjoying the view of the night sky, maybe thinking for a short time about Sweet Maria, but mostly thinking about that diner they had been in not too long ago. "Elk steak first," Bull said. "Then bear stew. Maybe an apple pie after."

"You forget something," Slim chuckled.

"Bottle or two of fine whiskey to wash it down." He looked over at Slim, tried his best to smile. "You should be proud of me, Partner."

"Oh? And just what should I be proud of, Bull?"

"I ain't got all riled up for two full days. Ain't like me."

"Getting old, Bull. Time to slow down. Retire and sit on the porch in a rocking chair, smoking a pipe, telling stories of the good old days."

"You sumbitch," Bull yelled out at the top of his lungs, set the spurs to tickling the horse's ribs, and the race was on. Pitch black, the most dangerous time to ride a horse at a full gallop, but the road was well used, there wouldn't be any badger holes, any high sage bushes, any rocks to trip over.

The men were leaning way out on the horse's necks,

split reins popping the horse's hips and flanks, screams of pure joy coming from both. "Bear stew," Bull howled.

"Elk hind quarter," Slim screamed.

It was other traffic in the early night that finally slowed the crazy marshals to a comfortable lope and finally down to a walk as they re-entered the town. Sweat ran down both men's faces, which quickly turned to ice, and they tied their tired horses off in front of the café. These were men who depended on their horses and they took the time to rub them down with rags from the saddle bags, and talking nice after such a hard ride.

"Beat you fair and square," Bull said, pushing his way through the heavy door into the diner. "Oh, yeah, fair and square."

"Damn near ran me in that ditch, Bull. That ain't fair and square. Forced me to evade that man and his wife in the carriage. That ain't fair and square."

"Let's have us a drink before supper, eh? That way you can pay off your losing bet."

Bet? Slim thought. He looked at Bull and had to chuckle. *This man I work for and with is a real piece of fine work. I don't think he's ever paid for a drink or a meal. Ever.*

The saloon half of the dinner house was filled with men enjoying the end of a long day. Some were state workers, some were elected officials, and Slim noticed, more than one seemed to be a gambler or a sharp. Most were in city clothes, cutaway coats, trousers without mud and blood stains, and many were not wearing weapons, at least not visible ones. Bull led them to the bar, pushed his way between two men and motioned for the barman.

"Easy, friend," one of the men said. "There's room for all."

"Damn right there is," Bull said. "Let's have some whiskey," he said to the barman. "Been one hell of a long day."

He and Slim clinked glasses and let the whiskey make its way all the way down. The iced blood was warmed, buffalo robe coats were untied and opened, and the night was pleasant. Warmth spread through the system and Slim took a long breath. "Glad we didn't have to finish that ride, Bull. I don't think either one of us would have enjoyed the end of it."

"Nope, we would not have. One more glass of this stuff and supper. Leave out at sunrise, eh? Get everything returned, and make for San Francisco." He almost spilled his drink and turned to the man next to him. Slim kept on talking.

"Leave out for San Francisco after the trial, Bull. We still have one prisoner left alive." Slim frowned, thinking about how this case had played out.

"Push me one more time, Mister, and I'll break your face into a million little pieces. I'm tired, cold, and hungry. Don't get me riled." He looked at Slim and tried his best to smile. Slim only sighed, waiting for the explosion. It came quickly.

"Shove?" the man said and swung his cane, which had a brass knob on the end of it, at Bull's head. Bull grabbed the finely turned walking stick, wrenched it from the man's hands, and broke it over his knee. He kept the half with the knob and slammed it into the man's head. The well-dressed man stood straight up at the hit, his eyes out of focus, and slowly fell to the floor. A trickle of blood eased its way across the boards.

There was immediate reaction from those standing closest but Bull's coat had opened and that shiny U.S.

Marshal's badge gleamed in the lamp light. "Man's got no manners," Bull said. "Gonna drink in a fine establishment like this, you must mind your manners." Was it the badge that kept the peace or was it Bull's size? Whatever it was, quiet settled over the scene to Slim's great surprise.

Bull laid the broken end of the cane on the bar, looked at the barman, and shook his head. "You cater to some rough hombres, Sir. Might have to think twice about drinking here in the future." He nodded to Slim and headed for the doors to the restaurant.

Slim laid a five-dollar gold piece on the bar, cocked his head a bit at the barman, and followed along. *There are times this man will completely destroy a saloon and other times he makes it an act of charity. I can't think of another man in the world I'd rather work for.*

CHAPTER 28

THE CAFÉ WASN'T CROWDED AND THE TWO BIG MEN TOOK a table for four. The young waiter saw to it that the tureen of elk stew was never empty. After he had filled it for the third time, Bull decided he was almost ready to face the rest of the night. "Only thing missing right now is a bottle of fine brandy and a big black cigar." He looked up toward the high ceiling. "The Italian ones, soaked in wine." Slim could see the reminiscing in his eyes, could almost smell the North Beach restaurants the two of them loved.

"Do you remember that place in North Beach where I got those horrible old cigars? They were ropes. Damn, but I do like them. Just as good to chew on as they are to smoke." Bull was warm and full and in an expansive mood. "Maglio's, that's it. Good steaks and good Italian cigars. First stop when we get home, eh, Slim?"

Slim had to chuckle watching Bull sit back in his chair as if he owned the place. "What are we going to tell the banker about the missing money if we're not going to chase Sweet Maria?" Slim said. Bull took that moment to look out the window. He let the question dangle about for a full five seconds.

"What missing money?" Bull said. "Did you count it? I didn't. Mike Duffy didn't."

Slim smiled watching the wily marshal. Clever, he thought. Bull Morrison was more than just a good lawman, he was empathetic as well, and was proving it at this moment. Ask him about it? He would deny it for hours, but Bull had a heart even if it was hard to find sometimes. Slim let the thought grow as he looked around.

A good lawman has to have a sense of right and wrong but also needs to show empathy as well. Too often the law isn't a simple black and white affair, it's many shades of gray. There are some who would say Bull is wrong letting Maria ride off with several hundred dollars of the bank's money. This is one of the cases of shades of gray.

"What's in the sacks is what we recovered," Slim said. *No,* he thought, *no one counted it, not even the banker. What we return is what we recovered. The working girl was giving up the profession and going home.* "Sometimes you have the biggest, softest heart of any man I've ever known, Bull Morrison."

"True story," Bull said. No argument, no denial, just that simple statement. Bull Morrison was his own man and you had to take him as he was because he liked who and what he was.

"We recovered two mules, a wagon, and feed sacks full of gold and silver coins that were stole from the Washoe City Bank," Bull said. "The gang that stole the loot is dead, the man that stole the loot from the gang is in custody. Near as I can tell, our job here in Nevada Territory is just about wrapped up."

"Still need to get Jake before a judge. Need to have him charged with taking part in the murder of Crazy Ned Paulson and his gang, the murder of the sheriff and his deputy, and the murder of those ranch hands.

"We ain't got a complete handle on the murder of Big Maude, either." Slim said. "Was it the two of them? Jake and Little Al?"

"I'll be glad to see Frank Oberlin," Bull said. "The work that man did? Amazing. Just think about being able to do that kind of work, Slim. Imagine getting those rocks, just so. That timber to look like it was natural for it to be where it was. I want to sit and talk to him for hours."

They brought a roasted chicken and boiled potatoes back for Duffy, a bottle of whiskey for Slim and a bottle of brandy for Bull, and settled in for the night on a bed of fresh straw at Jenkins' Stables on Roop Street, in Carson City, Nevada Territory.

"Too many people lost their lives, Bull," Slim said. "Too many. And all for a few bags of shiny metal."

"We always want to blame Jake for most of this," Bull said. He was sitting in the straw, leaning up against a wall, sipping his brandy straight out of the bottle. "It weren't Jake, Slim. Big Maude was behind the entire massacre. She set up Crazy Ned after he blabbed that they were going to be robbing the bank. Think about it, Slim. She let Crazy Ned know where the cabin was up Parker Canyon, then laid out the plan for Jake to ambush the gang. She directed Jake to ambush Paulson. The sheriff just got in the way."

"We'll hang Jake anyway," Slim chuckled. "He can't get away with saying something like, I was just doing what I was told to do."

Laughter rang through the rafters of the big barn and one of the mules picked that time to sound off, as well. "The clarion call of truth, right there," Bull said.

———

MIKE DUFFY DROVE the team of mules and Bull and Slim were the outriders on the long slow journey back to Washoe City. They pulled up in front of the stone courthouse and Sheriff Mockingbird Jessup came out to meet them. "Bank's gonna be mighty glad to get all that back in their vault. Where's the girl?"

"Had to let her go, Sheriff. Didn't even know what was in the wagon. Stole it to get away from the whorehouse. Recovered the wagon and mules, nobody filed any charges, no reason to keep her." Bull Morrison gave his little speech with a straight face, and Duffy and Slim found things to do to keep themselves busy while he spoke.

"How's our friend Jake holding up?" Slim asked.

"Not sure he's going to live but I did get some answers from him. He and Little Al planned the robbery of Big Maude's vault and it was Little Al who killed Maude, just as you thought, Bull. It was Jake who broke her arm, though. Only way he could get the combination to the lock."

"Yeah, tough guy, that Jake." Bull Morrison was ready to walk in the jail and take Jake's head off. "Don't think much of a man like that. She takes him in, gives him a good job, feeds him, and he breaks her arm to rob her of what he stole for her. Upstanding. Hang the bastard, I say."

"What about the Parker Canyon massacre?" Slim asked. "He say anything about that?"

Mockingbird shook his head. "Denied ever being there. I asked how he knew Big Maude had the loot in her vault and he shut up." There was a smile dancing its way across his rugged old face.

"Charges are filed on taking the money from Maude's vault and being an accessory to her death, but that's all I could get. He's the only one left alive," Mockingbird said. "County attorney is waiting for you and Slim so he can get his prosecution ready. I've give him all what I know. He wants the sacks of money to be put in the county vault until he can get a full count and then give it back to the bank."

"Ain't gonna let that bastard get off, get away with those fiendish killings at Parker Canyon," Bull said. He looked at Slim before continuing. "That Parker Canyon bloodbath has to be answered for, Slim, and that means we have to give the county one hell of a lot more than we have. You did good, Mockingbird. I'll take it from here."

"You've been busy, Mockingbird." Slim said. "All right, then, let's get this money put away, get the team tucked in, and have a huge meal. How is it we never stop to eat?"

"You ain't hungry," Bull said. "You're thinking of that pretty little girl." Slim just turned away and smiled. *Maybe so,* he thought. *Maybe so.* Bull stepped down from his horse and tied it off. "You and Duffy take care of that money, Slim, I'm going to take care of Jake James. Mockingbird, you stick close to me. I won't touch him but I'll put the fear of it close to his heart."

"He's in bad shape, Marshal. Doc Elroy has been checking on him regularly."

"I ain't gonna hurt him none," Bull said. He tried to smile but it wasn't in him. "He's already got the fear of Morrison in him. I'll just add some spice to that."

Jake was stretched out on his mattress in the tiny cell when Bull and Mockingbird walked in. "How you feelin' there, Jake James? Doctor Elroy said you're gonna live. Might be a bit sore climbing those stair steps, though," Bull said. He unlocked the cell, handed his revolver to the sheriff and walked into the cell.

Mockingbird relocked the door and Bull pushed Jake's legs aside and sat on the edge of the cot. "What stairs?" Jake asked. He groaned, trying to get into a sitting position.

"Why, the long stairs that lead up to the gallows, Jake. You're gonna hang, boy. Can't go around killing people and not pay the price." Bull was setting Jake up for a long and nasty, probably one-sided, conversation.

"I didn't kill nobody," Jake said.

"Well, now, let's talk about that. You told the sheriff that you broke Big Maude's arm so she would give you the combination to her safe and then you were with Little Al Tyson when he killed her. What you haven't told anyone is what you did out at Parker Canyon. Why, boy, that killing was a stroke of genius. Yes, sir, genius."

Jake sat up a little straighter and Mockingbird had to hold in a chuckle. *There's your genius,* he thought. *Ain't nothing Jake is gonna say that I don't already know but what I'm learning is the art of gettin' a man to be proud of the crime he's gonna hang for. Go get him Bull.*

"I didn't do it. It was Maude," Jake said.

"Maude did all that? Why, boy, it must have been

something. How did she do all that? Tell me. She had to have had help."

"I work for her. She told me what to do. It was all her idea."

Bull didn't say a word, just got up and walked to the bars, trying his best to smile. "Just like Slim said, eh, Sheriff?" Mockingbird cackled for a solid minute while Bull paced back and forth in the cell. Jessup was sure he was going to strike out and kill Jake but Bull had this little conversation in hand.

"Ain't never heard that much bullshit come out of one man's mouth. Never. You want me to believe that a big strong man like you killed all those people because a fat old whore told you to? You got guts enough to tell that to a judge?" He made another turn around the cell and sat down next to Jake. The man was bent over, staring at his feet, shaking.

"I ain't gonna hurt you, Jake," Bull said. "I'm gonna let the noose do that. Time to man-up, tell the truth, take responsibility for that massacre. You're gonna die for it, boy, might as well take responsibility for it."

Jake sat on the edge of the cot and the cell block was quiet except for the soft sobs that came from the man. "You ain't really a man, are you?" Bull snapped. "Married to a fat old whore who told you what to do, when to do it, even how to do it. You wanted to kill Paulson because he sent you to prison but couldn't even do that until that fat old whore told you how. Did she hold your hand while telling you how?"

Jake stiffened but couldn't do anything. He tried to jump to his feet, wanted to smash that foul mouthed marshal's head, but all he could do was groan when he tried. "Helpless little boy," Bull said softly. "Can't get even with the man who sent you to prison without being told how by your fat old whore wife. Does she hold your hand when you pee?"

"I did those killings, not Maude," Jake screamed. "I did them."

Bull looked over at Mockingbird who nodded back. "The sheriff is going to sit outside these bars, Jake, and I want you to tell him the whole story. Don't leave anything out. I'll know if you do and you don't want me back in here for a second session."

Mockingbird let him out, gave him his pistol back, and relocked the cell door. "Magnificent, Marshal. I coulda questioned Jake for days and not got all that. The county attorney is going to be one happy man."

Bull patted the sheriff on the shoulder and walked out of the jail area, grabbed his coat, and headed for Uncle Bob's Café.

CHAPTER 29

CELINDA O'MALLY WALKED UP TO SLIM, ALL FIVE FEET three inches of her, reached her arms around his neck, pulled him down and gave him a long, wet kiss as soon as he and Duffy walked into Uncle Bob's Café. "About time you got back, cowboy. My heart's been achin' and worryin something fierce."

He was startled first, then felt the excitement, and at the end of the kiss, thoughts of the future flooded the system. "Hungry, girl, then we'll talk some," he said. Her eyes were bright as he looked down on her pretty face, he felt the strength of her arms wrapped tight about his neck, and to make it worse, he thought, she smelled good. "Yes," he mumbled, "we'll talk some."

Duffy guffawed, whacked him across the shoulders, and marched to the table by the window. "Just start bringing food, darlin'. It's been one hell of a couple of days. You and Slim can sneak off after."

Bull joined up with them as they got settled in. "Don't know what you said, Duffy, but you got my partner pretty messed up right now."

Slim was beet red, Celinda was smiling, and Uncle Bob stuck his head out of the kitchen door. "She ain't goin' nowhere until after the dinner crowd."

"They got time," Duffy laughed. "We're gonna be in town until the trial's over."

"Enough!" Slim sat down, Celinda brushed her hand through his hair, and he scowled and smiled all at the same time. He looked up at those bright eyes, let his gaze come all the way down to her tiny little feet, and smiled some more. "I'll have the elk stew," he said, "for now."

It wasn't easy but Duffy got the conversation turned back on the subject of murder, robbery, and hanging. "Doc told Mockingbird that Jake was in bad shape. You think we're all but done around here? For me, I want to feel all that desert heat down in El Paso. I ain't cut out for cold. Not this kind of cold. Cold should be limited to beer." Duffy saw Bull nod in agreement, but what he said had nothing to do with beer.

"The county attorney is in charge right now," Bull said. "Jake gave it up with just a little prodding. Mockingbird's going to get all the details and give them to the attorney." He wanted a drink and settled for coffee. "A territorial judge will hear the case and we'll be set free," Bull said. "Ain't never worked something like this before, eh, Slim? Long as I live I'll never forget walking into the cabin up Parker Canyon and seeing all them bodies." He sat back in his chair, looking up at the ceiling, his eyes half closed.

Duffy groaned just a little, remembering when he walked into the cabin at the canyon. "You're right, Bull. All my years working this old badge and nothing's ever been as bad as that scene at the cabin. Don't never want to see something like that ever."

"Then we got to see all that beautiful work that Frank Oberlin did," Bull said. His eyes mellowed some, the fierceness was gone. "My God but he does fine work."

"The closest I've ever come to being creative like that is braiding rawhide," Slim said. "Nothing like what Oberlin does. You ever wanted to build something or make something?"

"Got a piece of maple wood once and thought I'd carve a handle for my knife. Ended up just a pretty piece of kindling when I got through," Bull said. "Ain't in me. We got a few days to go around here. Think I'll bother the hell out of old Frank Oberlin."

They were well into their meal when Mockingbird Jessup walked in and joined them. "Had to get Doc Elroy," he said. "Jake was making like he was dying. Doc says he was pretending. It might be best if one of you had a long talk with the man. I ain't sure it was pretending."

Bull turned and looked out the window at what was the start of a beautiful sunset. "Ain't it always the way, Slim? We got us all wrapped up, got some real beauty out there on that mountain top, and a damn outlaw has to come along and spoil things."

Bull looked at Mockingbird, then Slim, then Duffy. Signaled Celinda to come over, and took a sip of his coffee. "I simply ain't in the mood to ruin the end of this day. I'm so damn tired I might go to sleep walking back to the hotel. Duffy, we'll be through here in a day or two, so you need to make plans for getting back to El Paso."

He stopped, finished the coffee, and pointed a finger

at Slim. "You and this lovely lady have some unfinished business to take care of. I ain't gonna ruin the night by talking to Jake. He and I had our conversation. Sheriff, you got it all written down, so nothing to add to it.

"I'm gonna have a long sleep and tomorrow I'm going up to Doc's place and spend some time with Frank Oberlin. Jessup, you got questions for and about Jake, you handle it."

Bull stood up, grabbed his big coat and made for the door. "Take care of things, Slim."

"He will," Celinda said, loud enough for some still at nearby tables to hear. Slim reddened about the neck and ears, and Duffy laughed right out.

Celinda just smiled and rustled his hair about. "Uncle Bob and I had a little understanding, Slim, so when you finish your pie and coffee, we can take a little walk if you like."

He had a forkful of apple pie but made sure he hesitated long enough for her to bend down and give him a long kiss. "Anyplace in particular you'd like to walk to?"

"A very particular place," the lovely lady said. "And I'll have fresh coffee for you come sunrise."

Duffy sat quietly and watched the two put heavy coats on and walk out of the restaurant. "Don't much care for this gettin' older stuff," he murmured. *I'll be back in El Paso in a couple of weeks. Maybe it'll be time to give up this old badge, find me a pretty little Mexican girl and raise a mess of screaming kids. I ain't as old as Mockingbird, older than Bull Morrison, and young enough to love life.*

———

MOCKINGBIRD WAS SITTING at the sheriff's desk writing down everything Jake had said, and had a stack of papers filled with notes from the last many days. "I am one tired old man," he said right out, laying the quill next to the ink bottle. He got up to add another log to the wood burning stove when the county attorney walked in.

"Working late, eh Mockingbird? Got your note, saw your light and thought I'd stop in tonight instead of the morning. Good news, is it?" Roscoe Fillipini was in his mid-forties, married to a much younger woman who has given him a child and he's looking forward to his second. The thin, wiry, strong man bounced when he walked, outpacing the youngest men around the courthouse.

He was a prideful man and a bit of a rooster to boot. He wore wool pants, a white shirt with starched collar, and a brocade vest under a cut-away coat. His town shoes seldom had mud on them.

Fillipini was a tiger in the courtroom, had been approached more than once to stand for election to the territorial court system, but enjoyed the action of prosecuting outlaws. Politics wasn't his game. He was an athlete, excellent shot with rifle and pistol, and enjoyed the art of boxing. The punsters said his mama never taught him how to get tired.

"It is good news, Roscoe. I was in the jail with Marshal Morrison while he questioned Jake James about the Parker Canyon killings. I'll have this report finished before morning for you. He confessed to the whole thing. Tried to say he did it because Big Maude told him to."

Fillipini laughed. "Sounds like what a school boy

would say." He scowled and asked, "Did the marshal have to beat the confession out of him?"

"Never touched the man," Mockingbird said. "It was beautiful." He reached in that bottom drawer and brought the flask out. "Join me?"

"Just a short one, Mockingbird. Hortense has supper in the oven, I'm sure. You've done a fine job during all this uproar, Jessup. The county commission is wondering if you're going to stand for election. They have to call for that, you know."

"The sooner the better, too," Mockingbird said. "I ain't never worked this hard in my life." He made to wipe the sweat from his forehead and chuckled doing it. "No, Roscoe, I ain't standing for election. I'm retiring as soon as a new sheriff is elected. Don't even want to go back to being a jailer. Gonna find a big tree, sit under it, and smoke my pipe."

"There will be many more than I trying to tell you to stay on, Sheriff. I sent a note to Ed Crandle and he's going to represent Mr. James at his trial. Judge Hummings is coming up from Carson City to preside, so this mess is just about over."

"Glad for that. So many dead people. So much carnage. And all for a few thousand dollars. Ain't worth it, Roscoe. So many lives destroyed. The only man left alive is going to hang. Is that fitting?"

Roscoe Fillipini put the tin cup down, nodded but didn't say anything, and left Mockingbird to his own thoughts. "He's going home to a wife and warm house. I wonder what that's like?"

CHAPTER 30

MORNING SUN FOUND ITS WAY THROUGH HEAVY CURTAINS and feeble light to awaken Bull Morrison from a long night's sleep. He fought his way out from under a pile of blankets, noticed there was no one in the other bed and smiled. "Good for him."

Bull couldn't take his eyes off the scene from the hotel window. He wasn't quite all the way into his pants when he first looked out the window. All the snow from the past days stood out on the majestic Sierra Nevada ridges, brighter even than the sun itself. "My God all mighty would you look at that. Looks like I can just reach out and touch those mountains."

The lake was off to his left, the Sierra in front, and rolling hills covered in brilliant snow to his right. "Hard to be a morning grouch looking at that," he mused. "I like to start the day cussing at someone or something. Can't do it with all that beauty out there." The fact that there was ice in the wash basin didn't take away from the beauty of the scene. "No wonder Frank Oberlin finds such beauty in rocks and wood."

Even while dressing he took little sneak peeks out the window, giving his interpretation of a smile. His eyes smiled, though. *Every bone and muscle hurts. Been in the saddle for thirty years is what it feels like. Has been six days, though.* He let his mind work its way through those long days and couldn't break away from the scene at the Parker Canyon cabin. The ride over the crest of the Sierras was uneventful, as was the ride into Washoe Valley, but the Parker Canyon scene was hell in person.

All those bodies just thrown into the room and then froze in position. The worst part, Jake trying to say he did all that because some fat old whore told him to.

He was strapping on his gun belt when Slim walked in. "Well, now, looky here," Bull said. "Got yourself a goodly smile there, Slim old boy. Yes, sir, a goodly smile."

Slim wouldn't have been able to hide the smile even if he'd wanted to, and simply walked to the window to enjoy the view. "Ran into Mockingbird coming over. County attorney seems more than pleased with what you wrung out of Jake James. Judge will be here this afternoon, he said."

"Ain't nobody left alive except Jake so the trial should be short and sweet." Bull pulled his coat on, grabbed his hat and made for the door. "Supper last night did not fill all the holes, Slim. Looking for a pound of side meat and half a dozen eggs. Then we'll have breakfast."

The two fought and pushed each other getting down the stairs, laughing like two ten-year-old street urchins. "Ain't gonna race you, though," Bull said as they walked out on the street. "I'll meet you at Uncle Bob's. Gotta send a wire off to San Francisco and give the judge all the details of what we found here."

"Interesting, eh? Came all this way to finally put the iron on Singing Sammy and end up with bodies everywhere, criminal activity we had no business investigating, and at the end, one man in jail." Slim stood on the boardwalk shaking his head as Bull made his way to the telegraph office.

Slim went into the café and was swarmed by Celinda. Those watching were sure that she was equally swarmed, and it was several moments before the two separated and Slim made his way to a table. "Morning, Duffy. You're up bright and early."

"Slept like a baby, Slim. Dreams of El Paso, pretty Mexican girls, and maybe even retirement. This old badge is getting kind of heavy." His usually lively face looked tired, worn down, and his shoulders weren't quite as broad as yesterday's. "Maybe it's just the cold but I don't think so. Don't have a great desire to chase the bad boys, Slim."

"Couldn't do that, myself," Slim said. "Miss all this?" He spread his arms wide, taking in all of Washoe Valley and the Sierra Nevada. "No, as long as I'm physically capable, I'm gonna be a marshal." He took a drink of hot coffee and looked out the window at the high mountain ridges off to the west. "That's a wonderful view, Duffy, and imagine all the danger that's in it. That's our life, isn't it? Vile horrible people doing terrible things to each other while living in paradise. It's nice that we can take the time to see the beauty. I could live here."

"You have the makings of a fine poet, Marshal Calhoun," Duffy said. "I can see the beauty in those mountains, in the scene across Washoe Lake, but it's the stark beauty of the open desert that I miss. Those mountains around El Paso have one tree per square mile, maybe." He nodded toward the mountains. "I ain't never seen this many trees all in the same place. I could not be happy living here."

The men were in their own thoughts when Mockingbird walked up to the table with County Attorney Roscoe Fillipini. "Good morning," the sheriff said. "Where's Bull? Brought the county attorney to meet you boys. Also got some bad, maybe good news, too."

"What's that?" Slim asked.

"Mr. James died during the night," Fillipini said. "Seems the hurt those whores put on the man were more than enough to do him in. Won't be having a trial but I would like to have written reports from everyone involved."

"Here comes Bull, now," Duffy said. "Man walks like he owns the world, doesn't he?"

"He thinks he does," Slim chuckled. Celinda roughed up Slim's hair and moved to hold a chair for Bull. She wore a dazzling smile for the man.

"You are a charming little butterfly, my dear," Bull said. He turned to Fillipini. "And who might you be?"

"You must be Marshal Bull Morrison," Fillipini said. "I'm Roscoe Fillipini, County Attorney. Heard plenty of stories about you and Calhoun. Sheriff Jessup just informed us that our lone survivor had passed through the pearly gates."

"Probably just as well," Bull said. "We wouldn't have learned anything new if we did have a trial. Get all that money counted, did you?"

"Every penny, Marshal. It's in the vault at the bank now. No trial, so all I'll need is your reports and you're free to leave out, based on the weather, of course. Carson Pass and Donner Pass roads won't be open for weeks. Only way out of Nevada Territory is north to the Beckwourth Pass and down into the Sacramento Valley by way of Marysville."

"We'll be here another day or two," Slim said. "Mockingbird's going to put some heat on the men who rode for Little Al and those who backed up Jake. Told him we'd help if he needed it." Slim smiled at Celinda and got one back as she brought platters of pork chops, biscuits and gravy, and plates loaded with scrambled eggs.

———

CELINDA'S EYES told the real story. She knew where Slim stood as far as the marshal service went. He was a dedicated deputy and would not be a dedicated husband. They had talked about that during that long and wonderful night. He told her how difficult it would be to just ride off with Bull, sometimes for weeks at a time.

Her blood ran cold when he told her about some of their exploits, some of the men they had to subdue, some of the danger they faced so regularly. "I couldn't just ride off and leave you, Celinda, but that is a big part of my job."

"You could run for Washoe County Sheriff," she said but saw that wasn't the right thing to say. After an hour or two, they resolved to simply enjoy what time they would have together and not fight the obvious. Slim loved his job. He could love Celinda but it was his job that ruled.

Bull Morrison was the first to finish his breakfast

and was on his feet and in his heavy coat quickly. "You look like a man on a mission," Slim said.

"On my way to see Frank Oberlin. I'll get that report to you a little later, Fillipini."

Slim watched him slip out the door and wondered what the draw was for Bull to be this interested in Oberlin's life. *I've worked with that man for several years now and never seen him interested in anything other than either being a lawman or starting a brawl somewhere. I know he has a heart, I've seen shadows of it here and there, but this is different.*

———

BULL MORRISON WASN'T what one would call a deep thinker. He saw life most often in black and white. Seldom were there shades of gray, so this interest in what Frank Oberlin did with rocks and timber was exceptional. "Ain't got a good night's sleep because of you, Mr. Oberlin," he said, settling into a comfortable wing back chair next to Oberlin's bed. Doctor Elroy wasn't pleased with the early visitor but Oberlin said it was fine with him. At the mention of Marshal Bull Morrison's name, when the doctor told him of a visitor, Frank Oberlin's first thoughts were of that first visit at the Lakeside Inn. *Just what does that angry and mean looking man want now? Didn't even say hello, just said I was responsible for something or other.*

"And just why would that be, Marshal?" He was in pain but did what he could to not show it. Bruises would go away at some point, broken bones would heal. Just what was this marshal up to?

"The work you do, sir. I've seen fine woodwork

before, after all, my home is in San Francisco. But you've added something, something that I can't describe yet can see plainly. What you've done with some rocks and pieces of wood is sheer artistry."

The two men, so different in so many ways, yet drawn by the manipulation of some stones and timber. Oberlin just as big and strong as Bull, having worked in the forests as a log cutter, and then in the mills moving huge lengths of raw timber into the spinning saw blades. *Most interesting,* Frank thought. *Maybe I misjudged the man. Maybe there's more to this angry man than what seems obvious.*

"What do you do with your time when you're not chasing crooks, Marshal? I draw pictures of what I want my forest inn to look like. I've spent years making those pictures better and better, and when I found myself in Washoe City, surrounded by incredible timber and massive amounts of Sierra granite, I built what I drew."

"You make it sound rather simple," Bull said. He sat back and thought about the question Frank asked. "What do I do when I'm not chasing crooks? Damn, Frank, I really don't know. Never have given something like that a thought." *What do I do? I visit every restaurant I can find.* He chuckled and looked at Oberlin.

"I go to saloons and start fights and I go to restaurants and eat everything offered." The realization came slow, ploddingly slow. "I don't have a life outside being a marshal." The thought wasn't the least bit friendly. *I'll be damned. I'm not ashamed of how I live, but Oberlin's life seems so much better.*

"I've had a dream since I was a boy, Marshal. I think your dream is wonderful. You're an upstanding and successful lawman. Men look up to you. People are safe because of you. Your dream is a bit more substantial than mine, I think." Frank Oberlin smiled and laid his head back on a soft pillow. "My dream is rock hard. Yours has a different form of substantial."

Frank looked at Bull and saw a fierceness that he would never have, yet he also saw that Bull thought there was something missing. "Other than fighting and eating, do you have any kind of hobby?"

"Hobby? What the hell would that be? Hobby? Who has time for something like that? No, I don't."

"That's how my Lakeside Inn came about. I loved playing with rocks, making fence lines, rock walls as a youngster. My grandfather taught me how to work with wood, particularly big timber. It was his business, but it was my hobby," Frank said.

"Catching bad guys is all I've ever wanted to do. I was a boy, young as hell when I first met a man wearing a badge. My brother was scared, I remember, but I wasn't. I wanted one right that moment. Wore my first one when I was eighteen years old." He reached up and brushed the badge as if it was dusty, caught himself, coughed softly and sat quiet.

"You're a work of art, Bull Morrison," Frank said. "Thank you."

"Thank me? What for?"

"Well, for starters, thank you for saving my life," he laughed. "How's that? And for solving all those murders. And for getting the bank's money back. And for being you. I think we're going to be friends for a long time, Bull. I like that idea."

"I do, too," Bull said, ever so quietly. "You've got me thinking now about a hobby. What would it be, I wonder?" Bull looked down at his huge hands, gnarled from years of fighting, working with rifles and pistols, taming the bad guys. They weren't pretty. He chuckled softly when he glanced at Oberlin's hands and saw just about the equal.

"You and me are tough guys, Frank, but you've brought a form of beauty into the world I don't think I could do. You'll have me thinking, though. About a hobby, that is."

They spent another half hour discussing Oberlin's building of the Lakeside Inn, about Jake James and Little Al Tyson, and Big Maude. "Doc is sending me back home in the next day or so. Please stop by, bring that young partner of yours, and we'll chat some more."

"I'll do that, Frank. Get well." They shook hands and Bull made his way out, already trying to think of what it would be that he would enjoy spending time doing. Other than fighting and eating. "I like fighting and eating," he muttered, heading to town.

CHAPTER 31

"YOU READY TO GO HOME? I SURE AM," BULL MORRISON said. The two men were leaving the Washoe County courthouse on a brisk afternoon. "What did Mockingbird call you back about?"

"Seems the ownership group at The Timbers has filed a complaint with the sheriff about Big Maude's Pleasure Palace. They're operating day and night but apparently without an owner."

"Good for them," Bull laughed. "And sifting money away from The Timbers. Dastardly offensive, Slim. Frighteningly horrible. Must seriously affect their bottom line at that fine saloon. What's Mockingbird going to do about it?"

"That man has been wasting his life these last many years working as a jailer. As you've said, he should have been the sheriff all along. There has been no one come forward to claim what Big Maude owned or what Jake James owned. Big Maude owned the building and the license was in Jake's name. Get the picture?"

"It's coming into focus, Slim. He put in a claim on the land and the license, eh? That little devil."

"Yup. He said that it just came to him that he should run the joint and he had no idea that the claim would be honored."

Bull snorted. "You mean like a mining claim? Ain't never heard of such a thing. Can't be legal."

"Mockingbird Jessup wrote up a claim based on abandoned property, filed it with the territorial judge who granted the property to the old man," Slim laughed. "He ain't gonna change much. The name stays the same. Who would visit 'Mockingbird's Pleasure Palace?' he said." They both laughed at the thought and Slim continued. "He's already hired a crew to clean the place up, add some life to the joint."

"Washoe County is the loser here, then. The county would be better off if he ran for sheriff," Bull said. He got contemplative, spent a few moments looking at his boots. "And, my friend, what are you going to do?"

"Have a drink at The Timbers with you and discuss making plans for our trip home over the Sierra Nevada. Join me?"

They pushed and shoved each other each trying to be first through the bat-wing doors, laughing like misbehaving ten-year-olds. They caught the attention of those in there but nobody had guts enough to challenge the marshals. Some had seen Bull Morrison in a fight or two, and others had heard the stories. Rowdy behavior by two men wearing badges kept the place rather quiet.

"How about bringing a bottle and glasses to our table, barman? Me and my deputy got some work to do. Better bring a couple of cold beers, too," Bull snarled, but his eyes were full of life, even a touch of mirth.

"Must have been a good visit with Frank Oberlin," Slim said. "How's he feeling?"

"Ready to go home, he said. We talked about having a hobby. You got a hobby?"

"Don't think so. You?"

"Nope," Bull laughed. "Told Frank my hobby was fighting and eating. Why don't you have one?"

"Too busy being a deputy marshal, I guess." Slim was about to take a long drink of chilled beer when a large man, dressed as a drover, pushed him hard, spilling beer down his front. "Watch it, mister," Slim said, starting to get up.

He was slow and Bull wasn't. Morrison was on his feet, his fists swinging, driving the man back where he bounced off the rocks of the fireplace. A hard left to the man's nose followed by a strong right, low to the man's front side, and the fight was over. "You'd be wise to learn your manners," Bull said, jerking the man to his feet. "That wasn't an accident. You went out of your way to knock that beer over."

Bull walked him to the table, saw a gleam in the man's eyes, knew he was going to be stupid, and watched a clumsy attempt to grab for his weapon. "Damn me, but you are ignorant," Bull said, pile driving a fist into the man's kidneys, dropping him back to the floor. He was writhing in pain, trying desperately to catch his breath.

"They don't teach kids nothin' today, do they Slim? Man's just a slob." Bull relieved the cowboy of his weapon, got him on his feet, and slammed him into a chair. "Now, you ignorant sumbitch, what was that all about? You got less than five seconds to start talking or you won't have any teeth to talk through. Let's start with a name, eh?"

"Johnny Bigelow," he said. He was wheezing from that vicious kidney punch, wouldn't sit up straight, and Bull was ready to let him have another wild right to the head. Slim called him off.

"Let him try to talk, Bull. Might be something behind this."

"Well, Johnny Bigelow, that was a dumb thing to do. You got yourself all bruised up, bloody, too, and now you can tell me why you got all rowdy with a Deputy U.S. Marshal." Bull waited almost a full second. "Well?" The slap across the side of the man's head could be heard half a block away, and the cowboy's head flopped back and forth a time or two before falling to the table.

Half a dozen men standing at the bar all took in a deep breath thinking how glad they were that it was Bigelow taking the slap. Not a one gave any thought to coming to Bigelow's aid.

"Don't think he wants to talk to you, Bull. Must be something in your manner."

The barman walked over with a fresh beer for Slim. "Don't know what brought all this on, but that's Little Al's young brother."

"I thought Little Al was a Tyson? Bull said.

"Different fathers," the barman said. "Tyson's father died in prison and his mother married Bigelow. He's in jail down in Carson City as we speak. This boy here will spend some time in prison before he's twenty."

"He ain't bright," Slim laughed. Bigelow moaned and tried to sit up straight. "Glad you decided to join the party. I take it you're upset about your brother's death. Sorry for that but it was Jake that killed him, not us.

You're a hot-headed little punk kid, sonny. Change your ways or you'll be resting in that cold ground alongside Mr. Tyson."

"It's prison time to attack a federal officer, kid." Bull was right in his face, that horrible scar a bright red gash across his face. "Three to five would be my guess."

"Don't think he'd live to get out, Bull," Slim said. "Gonna do you one big favor, sonny. Gonna shove your skinny ass out that door and send you home to mama. If either Marshal Morrison or I see you, you'll either go to prison or to hell, your choice."

Bull jerked him to his feet, marched him to the swinging doors, and flung him through, face-first. There were some comments from those outside and some laughter from those arrayed along the bar inside. "You like my hobby, Slim? I do."

"Weather's got a nice feel to it," Slim said. "Let's leave out in the morning, eh?"

"Ain't gonna say goodbye to that sweetie of yourn?"

"Did," Slim said. Bull looked at him and knew better than to say anything else. Slim had made a hard decision that didn't need any comments, sly or otherwise from him.

A LOOK AT: NEWCOMERS

BROOKSIDE, OREGON TERRITORY
BOOK TWO

The Oregon Territory village of Brookside sees further violence as the lone constable fights to keep law and order in the second novel in the continuing series of life during Oregon's wild frontier period.
The year is 1848. The place is Brookside, Oregon Territory. The great migration from east to west is just getting underway following favorable comments on Oregon weather, farming, and ranching land in the eastern press. There are those in the Brookside Valley who are dead set against the immigrants. There are those who favor the movement. And there are those who take advantage of the newcomers. Worst of all, good people die.

The Brookside constable's office is a one-man affair, and Constable Kennedy is alone as the population explodes, crime explodes, and he is denied the ability to hire deputies. Some of his time is taken up by the delightful Widow Creighton.

The one man standing in the way of Constable

Kennedy getting help is beaten, robbed, and killed, and Kennedy is blamed. It's a big question whether he will survive this attack on his reputation.

AVAILABLE NOW

ABOUT THE AUTHOR

Reno, Nevada novelist, Johnny Gunn, is retired from a long career in journalism. He has worked in print, broadcast, and Internet, including a stint as publisher and editor of the Virginia City Legend. These days, Gunn spends most of his time writing novel length fiction, concentrating on the western genre. Or, you can find him down by the Truckee River with a fly rod in hand.

Made in United States
North Haven, CT
15 June 2023

37762995R00157